George Francis Armstrong

Mephistopheles in Broadcloth : A Satire

George Francis Armstrong

Mephistopheles in Broadcloth : A Satire

ISBN/EAN: 9783744734950

Printed in Europe, USA, Canada, Australia, Japan

Cover: Foto ©Andreas Hilbeck / pixelio.de

More available books at **www.hansebooks.com**

MEPHISTOPHELES IN BROADCLOTH.

POETICAL WORKS OF GEORGE FRANCIS ARMSTRONG.

MEPHISTOPHELES IN BROADCLOTH: A Satire. Fcap. 8vo. Price 4s.

STORIES OF WICKLOW. Fcap. 8vo. Price 9s.

A GARLAND FROM GREECE. Fcap. 8vo. Price 9s.

POEMS: LYRICAL AND DRAMATIC. A New Edition. Fcap. 8vo. Price 6s.

UGONE: A TRAGEDY. A New Edition. Fcap. 8vo. Price 6s.

KING SAUL. (The Tragedy of Israel, Part I.) Fcap. 8vo. Price 5s.

KING DAVID. (The Tragedy of Israel, Part II.) Fcap. 8vo. Price 6s.

KING SOLOMON. (The Tragedy of Israel, Part III.) Fcap. 8vo. Price 6s.

VICTORIA REGINA ET IMPERATRIX: A JUBILEE SONG FROM IRELAND, 1887. Price 2s. 6d.

BY THE SAME AUTHOR.

THE LIFE AND LETTERS OF EDMUND J. ARMSTRONG. Fcap. 8vo. With Portrait and Vignette. Price 7s. 6d.

EDITED BY THE SAME AUTHOR.

THE POETICAL WORKS OF EDMUND J. ARMSTRONG. A New Edition, containing poems not before published. Fcap. 8vo. With Portrait on Steel by JEENS, and Vignette. Price 5s.

ESSAYS AND SKETCHES OF EDMUND J. ARMSTRONG. Fcap. 8vo. Price 5s.

LONGMANS AND CO.

MEPHISTOPHELES

IN

BROADCLOTH:

A SATIRE.

BY

GEORGE FRANCIS ARMSTRONG,

M.A., D.LIT.

" Il y a dans les discours de Méphistophélès une ironie infernale
qui porte sur la création tout entière, et juge l'univers comme un
mauvais livre dont le diable se fait le censeur."—DE STAËL.

" The Enemy, like a modern gentleman,
Still walks the earth with hungry ears. Beware ! "

LONDON:

LONGMANS, GREEN, AND CO.

AND NEW YORK: 15 EAST 16th STREET

1888.

MEPHISTOPHELES IN BROADCLOTH.

I 'M somewhat weary, and a little sick,
  Of wandering through this wilderness of brick ;
But here is Rotten Row, a famous place
Where worn-out London flaunts its *blasé* face ;
And here the meanest man that wears a coat
May see the world go by him for a groat. . .
Dear blooming beauties ! . . Let me take a chair,
And sit with idle gentlemen, and stare. . .

It is not oft allowed me for a spell
To quit the lower for the upper hell,
Yet Evil's ends are satisfied as well—

B

The world, I find, on looking round about me,
Goes to the Devil very well without me.

But, recently, by some mysterious shove,
The trap-door opencd, and I came above ;
And, though by gouty conscience still annoyed,
My little holiday I 've much enjoyed.
" Dear are the pleasures that are dearly earned ; "
And many things I 've noted, many learned.
So fast in Error's way these mortals go
By their example we 'll progress below.

So much I 've seen that, as 't is fashionable
For every babbler now to print his babble,
If I remain but three weeks more from home,
I also will produce a parchment tome.
I 'll print my observations line for line
So that the " reading public " here may see 'em,
And get 'em lauded in the A ———m
By asking in the Editor to dine.

'T is said to be outlandish now 's the way

To make your literary offspring pay.

But there are other crutches quite as mean

Whereon your lame and limping authors lean,—

As, joining some close clique or corporation

Banded to palm its produce on the Nation

And from Fame's temple carefully exclude

All writers of an independent mood—

Some mutually-congratulating club

Of poetasters, let us say, who snub,

Or patronize with condescending sneer,

At social gatherings where they most appear,

Or in the pages of their pet Reviews,

All bards that homage to the ring refuse. . .

By Heaven! I 'll join a clique, the strongest faction

That draws the pressmen close with prime attraction,

Belaud the "great" among them, soothe the small,

Adore, delight, uphold, oblige them all,

Then launch my book, and in a trice arise

A leading author borne aloft on lies.

No better road to fame could I propose.

Whether I clothe my thoughts in verse or prose

Is doubtful.   Every man 's now called a poet

Who has a trumpet and a clique to blow it.

The name of poet 's hardly worth the seeking

Where every room with poetlings is reeking,

And every table with their volumes creaking.

True poets are a most unhappy race,

And oft their loftiest finds the lowest place.

I pity them—the proud and tender creatures—

Because they must with hard-grained tradesmen
      deal,

With publishers of stern and icy features,

With butchers, chandlers, readers cold as steel,

The wretch that spoils their houses he upholsters,

Tailors whose bills are needles in their bolsters,

And—sharper to the touch than lancewood
      splinters—

The printer's devils and the devil's printers.

A cheese breeds maggots and a poet critics ;

They stick as close as words and their enclitics.
Critics, those knaves of most obnoxious noses
That seem for ever conscious of queer smells
Where healthier people sniff the breath of roses,
Against their ban in vain the bard rebels.

Yet, were a choice of crowns before me laid,
I'd choose the true bard's bays—they never fade.
I have a kindly leaning toward the tribe;
They have a kindly leaning, too, toward me;
And I am mindful of the smallest bribe
And faintest tribute to my vanity.
My name for ever ornaments their page,
I've been their brightest hero many an age,
And still I linger on the lyric stage.
I'm very grateful to divinest Dante,
And Virgil who with most benign intent
Led him enraptured through my many ante-
Chambers, and taught him tortures to invent,
Which since I've taken under my protection,

And find they suit my system to perfection.

To that grey edifice the Church of Grace

I also owe a thousand thousand thanks

For giving me so prominent a place

Among the sacred histrionic ranks

Of priests, disciples, dogs like Pontius Pilate,

Gay publicans no pharisee will smile at,

Barabbases, weak Peters, Caiaphases,

Judases, Josephs, cocks, and colts, and asses,

That throng the scenes of mediæval plays,

And in the midst of whom, in holier days,

To coax the erring in her fold to dwell,

She deemed my presence indispensable,

So taught the bards my features to descry

And keep me alway in the public eye.

To whomso first devised the goodly tale

Of Faustus too my hymns will never fail.

Then that sublime boy-poet, Shakespeare's master,

Whose life was dashed with premature disaster,

Poor Kit, the victim of a Deptford knife

Raised to avenge a sweetheart or a wife,

Slain in the morn of glory, youth, and pleasure,

Immortal Marlowe, whose heroic measure

Rolls like the voice of waters on the ear—

He to my heart of heart as light is dear.

To him his land owes much, and I no less;

He clothed me in the neatest-fitting dress.

But daily do I homage to thy name,

O serene Milton, who, in spite of shame,

Exaltest me for ever! When I read

Thy page my heart doth inly pine and bleed,

My spirit writhes in that fell agony

That heaved it in proud warfare to defy

The Eternal and disturb His tranquil reign,

And back returns the old remorseful pain.

Immortal Goethe in immortal song

Makes me immortal, but he makes me wrong;

I am not half the mean thing that he paints,

Nor half so clumsy when I tempt the saints;

Indeed I seldom wander from my lair

To goad a rascal or a saint to snare;

I set the ball a-rolling long ago,

And Evil reigns though I remain below.

Yet to the Doctor I am much indebted;

The appetite for sin he somewhat whetted;

Some morals that he taught us I approve—

Men should be cruel to the things they love,—

That is, they should do with them what they please,

And study nothing but their own vile ease.

It well avails me, works an equal evil,

That men should worship Self as serve the Devil.

So, though he made me half contemptible,

I like Herr Doctor Goethe passing well;

I profit by the prominence he gave me,

And thank him for much trouble he will save me.

But most of all love I your music, Burns,

Sad, gay and fierce and delicate by turns.

"Auld Nick" himself wept o'er your dying head

And sighed to soothe the roughness of your bed.

Ah Burns, poor thrall of love and joyous revel,

Whate'er the Kirk may swear to be your due,

The Devil never can be hard on you

Who could not ev'n be hard upon the Devil!

Others have worshipped me, but none like these

Whose homage was the heart's and not the
　　　knee's ;

For Coleridge, while he loved not Evil, drew

With Southey's help my face of such a hue

That none who know me by the picture crude

Will shrink from meeting me in solitude ;

And Byron, while he served me faithfully

Through six-and-thirty years of ribaldry,

Did little to advance my tarnished fame,

And trifled with my venerable name ;

And Shelley, that frail soul so weak and winning,

Too guileless to perceive when he was sinning,

Blaspheming God for making me and Hell,

Deemed each a myth, though writing *Peter Bell*. . .

I had forgot a book that once oppressed us,—

That endless Festus Bailey's " Bailey's *Festus*,"

And *Golden Legends,* and a score of other
Books that much sense in needless metre smother...

Enough! The bards have honoured me, and given
The critics thoughts whereby their pens have
    thriven.
At Edinburgh I said, "Before I pass on,
I 'll call upon the Scottish critic Masson,
And ask him, in a deferential tone,
Which of the devils now I most resemble,—
Luther's, or Milton's, Goethe's, or his own."
Even the Devil at critics well may tremble.
I called.   His face was frigid as a stone.
Reception could not ever colder be.
His would be warmer should he visit me.

If by a preëstablished harmony
I and the poets ever thus agree,
Should I attempt a book, I 'd best begin it
In verse.   No matter then if nothing 's in it;

It will the more resemble Swinburne's art—

" Form for form's sake,"—no jam inside the tart,—

To pass away like fashionable slang

Or bubbles blown by Mallock or by Lang,

Or rondeaux, sonnets, Provençal confetti

Still served up by the rump of the Rossetti ;

Ay, though I fail to join a clique, or scorn

Some influential pressmen to suborn,

To cite reviews yet know the man who wrote 'em

Is just my own paid agent and *factotum,*

And though I ogle every Muse in vain,

I yet might touch the skirts of Gosse or Payne. . .

This gentleman hard by is such a prater

He must be some distinguished legislator.

Ah ! yes, I've grown familiar with the species,

And know an eagle when among the geese he is.

I said, " In London I shall not omit

To see the Commons when the Commons sit."

I wished to watch them, with no purpose sinister,

So dropt a postcard to far-famed Minister,

Requesting of that pillar of the State

Simply an Order for the next Debate.

He sent an answer, but so strangely penned it

The more I read the less I comprehend it.

I cannot say that it is not effusive ;

'T is only somewhat nebulous and elusive :—

" Dear Sir,—I have received your note with pleasure

And read enough to see that at more leisure

The rest of it I shall not read in vain.

'T is clear the Tory moon is on the wane.

I think our common cause is wholly just.

In Providence I trust you put your trust.

Thanks for your interest in this Great Nation.

You have my prayers and best consideration."

I waited for the Order, but it came not.

And yet his ways ambiguous I blame not.

I am not of his party.   Still he knows me

Too well to know not that he something owes me.

I taught him much, while yet he needed teaching ;

Taught him to preach, not follow his own
    preaching;
Taught him that use of words he knows so well,
Nothing to leave unsaid, yet nothing tell;
Taught him to wear his conscience on his sleeve,
Deceive the Nation and himself deceive;
To read the Book in Church on Holy Days,
And when a Hero dies go see the plays;
Before the sacred Table bend the knee,
And never to forgive an enemy;
To flirt with faction, cut the State adrift,
Protest, explain, dodge, dive, elude and shift,
Eat his own words, and palter every hour,
On his own broken pledges climb to power,
Ignore his Queen, and, clad in saint's attire,
Drag his vexed country daily through the mire.
And so I do n't think he should play the actor
With his best friend and oldest benefactor.

But access to the Commons may be gained

By many ways that need not be explained.

Few know me when not clothed in black and red,

And fewer when the horns are off my head;

Ev'n preachers threatening Satan with most fell

    bow

Do n't see him when he 's standing at their elbow;

So, passing for some Judge with state-paid salary,

I entered the Distinguished Strangers' Gallery,

And, sitting by a Rajah in that place,

I looked quite white beside his heathen face.

Who flouts the name of England, who ignores

Her banners waving o'er a thousand shores?

What foe that ever with her prowess fought

The tempests of her onsets has forgot,

Or doubts the courage of her stubborn sons,

And cowers not at the thunder of her guns?

Who fails the might of intellect to trace

In Shakespeare's, Milton's, Newton's, Darwin's

    race?

Who deems her noblest energies are dead,

And every virtue from her heart hath fled?

Not I; and yet that senatorial show

Might lay the pride of all her children low.

There Britain's third-rate minds at dead of night

Or on, half-dozing, through the dawning light,

Exhausted, maddened with the unearthly noises

And howling hurricane of Irish voices

('Mid which I heard the Speaker called a rogue

By someone shrieking in a Galway brogue),

Confused and addled, careless what they said

If only they could get at last to bed,

Were forging, in rage, hate and panic blended,

The laws whereon the Empire's fate depended! . .

But this was some time since. Now all is changed.

The Commons' House in order is arranged! . .

Fall of the Mighty!—O, that ye should need your

Successive stringent New Rules of Procedure!

The Public Houses close here at eleven—

The Commons' one hour later! . . O great Heaven!

Where is the Saxon's boasted self-restraint,

The temperate calm his poets loved to paint?

What fate degrades him or what cruel chance,

That he must go for curbs and gags to France?..

I gazed upon six hundred languid faces

Of legislators lolling in their places,

And sought in vain amid their ranks unblest

For England's wisest and for England's best.

Some honest folk among them I could note,

Just men who might as conscience bade them vote;

Some stately souls that could not stoop to brawl;

Some nobles that could more than yawn and
 drawl;

Some hats that rested not on empty heads;

Some reputations not yet torn to shreds;

Some graceful Plunkets 'mid the wild O'Triggers;

Some Brights amid the Bradlaughs and the Biggars.

But where were England's thinkers? Where the
 men

That wield in pure devotion sword or pen?

Where were the patriot souls that seek alone

Their country's weal and care not for their own?

Far from the Senate's purlieus seemed to stand

The noblest and the ablest of the land;

The strong, the God-made rulers of the realm

Renounced, and let the unworthier seize, the helm,

Cast statecraft and ambition to the winds,

And left the loathsome game to lower minds.

I murmured not at this.   It gladdened *me*. . .

Speed, speed the ruin, O Democracy!

Yes, round about the Witches' Cauldron go;

Pour in the ingredients; let them ranker grow.

Pour in the place-hunter whose wrongs are righted

If even he can boast that he's been knighted;

The craftier knave of more ambitious aim,

Content to crawl through sewers and sinks of
        shame,

In hope to gain a seat among the Peers

By eating mud through half-a-score of years,

Then stalk in robes and mimic dignity,

A full-fledged peer with purchased pedigree;

Pour in the Jew that covets an alliance

With noble lords who greedily affiance

(For gold dishonouring an ancient stem)

Their daughters to the sallow sons of Shem;

The lawyer next on selfish ends intent,

Who holds the House a ladder of ascent,

A rung, to clasp with momentary clench

Of hasty hands up-clambering to the Bench,

Who at the hustings vows his one desire

Is just to serve the State through flood and fire,

But ere his hustings speech has left the press

Issues his "valedictory address;"

Pour in the pimp, the publican, the sinner,

The grimy tramp that begs or steals his dinner,

The law-defier using as a hedge

His lofty legislator's "privilege,"

The houseless lodger lately made a voter,

Content till now to breakfast on a bloater,

The burglar fattening on his neighbour's ale,

The shaven convict just emerged from jail ;

Pour in the whole bad brood become notorious

By doing things outrageous and uproarious,

Till old King Mob his final feat achieves,

The House of Commons is a den of thieves.

Then let the once proud Empire, weak and blind,

Ruled by brute motives and a drunkard's mind,

Lame, staggering, mocked by every whiffler's breath,

Reel down through degradation to its death. . .

Sweet consummation ! . . Nay, shall Good prevail,

And I once more in schemes of ruin fail ? . .

But see, a stir is yonder ! It might seem

Just a mere ripple on a tranquil stream.

The quiet people softly move aside

And leave the carriage-ways a moment wide,

And many turn a little round to see

Who 's coming through this concourse of the free.

It is the Prince. They like him. That is clear.

The languid faces lighten far and near.

An English Prince, an English gentleman,

Kind, genial, brave.   I heard the cheer that ran

Gathering from hill and vale and field and street,

When England's loyal hosts arose to greet

Their Sovereign's firstborn son, from tightening hand

Of Death snatched back to grace his native land,

As to the temple of the Living God

Beside his Royal Mother good he rode,

To thank the Power that stayed him from the grave;

A shout that like the thunders of the wave

Rolling upon the stormy Labrador

Echoed around her Empire's leagues of shore.

I heard it in my murky halls, and knew

Death's aims were baffled, and my longings too.

I yearned to see destruction in the Isle,

The triumph of my most insidious guile,

A race of children nursed on Besant's milk,

The Church of Bradlaugh and the State of Dilke.

My hopes were dashed, as oft before they 'd been;

England, still loyal to her peerless Queen,

Would guard the sacred treasure of her throne,

And yearn for law-fenced liberty alone.

Pass, Albert Edward, welcomed as you go

By every wholesome heart of high and low,

Prince, nursing no ambition in your breast

Except to see your Isle content and blest,

Foremost in every gentle deed of grace,

Gladdening the crowd with ever kindly face ! . .

On all sides round my traps are laid to lame him,

And if his foot should stumble, who shall blame

     him ? . .

  Ah year propitious ! Happy celebration

Of that which, 'mid Earth's boons that flame and

     fleet,

Looks fairest in my heart's great desolation,—

Marriage,—of human lives the union sweet,

Love's perfect, tenderest, holiest harmony ! . .

Again the land rejoices. Many a knee

Is bent in prayer before that loftiest Throne

To which all bow whose hearts are not as stone,

To beg that endless blessings still may shower,—

Albert and Alexandra,—grace and power,

Glory and peace, upon your wedded lives! . .

O gentlest, fairest of all England's wives,

If it were mine to bless, could I to-day

Remember thy bright marriage-morn, nor pray,

As England prays, that every wind that blows

May bear thee life and strength, sweet Danish

rose . .

Think they I never know remorse or sorrow

For griefs of men from which my strength I borrow—

Ay, pain on pain to feel that out of Pain

Alone my fruitless triumphs I must gain?

It is my doom to mock—no curse were fitter;

But evermore the mocker's joys are bitter. . .

Certes, this *is* a pleasant place to sit,

And watch the human frailties round me flit.

Lo, now, among the umbrellas and the sticks,

There struts the Bantam-Cock of Politics—

Spurs sharp as steel and beak made keen for fight

And blood-red comb and plumage fiery-bright!

Too weak too lead, too fractious to be led,

Already half his flickering glory's fled—

The press-proclaimed ambassador to Russia,

Boxed on the ears, in passing home, by Prussia;

Yearning to leave on history's page just *his* mark,

He gains for guerdon a rebuff from Bismarck.

Foiled in his hope his Leader still to lead,

He stabbed his party in its hour of need,

And earned the cold curt comment of his Chief,—

"Goodbye, dear Schoolboy—(Thanks for this
    relief.)"—

I almost chuckled when I read that Letter;

Disraeli, or myself, could frame no better—

A huge sledge-hammer driving home a nail;

A grain of barley flattened by a flail.

Yes, with the tyro chief compare the Master,

The true-born Premier with the premier-aster—

The One prepared to risk the Vessel's weal

In his hot haste to meddle with the wheel;

Prepared to see the Ship to ruin go

Rather than serve in peace and keep below;

Or see her flung from billowy ridge to ridge

If he himself could stand not on the bridge;

The Other willing, would it help the State,

To toil, a rival chief's subordinate—

A ruler planning only what might prove

Best for his country, not his own self-love;

A ponderous mind, not made for show or speed—

Not a lithe horse, like Dizzy (wingèd steed!),

Or young rogue Randolph few but fools will trust,

Or Gladstone backing in a cloud of dust;

Rather a traction-engine, huge and broad,

Clattering with rough hard wheels along its road,

Good to crush stones with, not to leap or race,

Do useful work, but do it without grace. . .

Hold, hold!—I cry with Goldsmith's Marlowe
    here,
"No, hang it! no, I won't be too severe!"
When up in London for a holiday
Asperity will never be my way.
I grant the little Ishmaelite is clever,
Most capable of strenuous endeavour,
Courageous, quick of stroke, and keen of wit,
For dashing charges eminently fit,
Industrious, oftener rich than poor in tact,
A colt that never bucks if never backed.
With more of conscience and with less of vanity
His future may not prove a sad insanity. . .

I envy these great English, I confess,
Their fire-concealing vast impassiveness.
Last night upon a platform, mute and meek,
I sat to hear the Coming Premier speak.
The people rose and cheered the Cavendish.
Callous he stood, and gelid as a fish.

Then, when he spoke, each sentence seemed to
    pass

Like some huge serpent moving through thick
    grass,

Still onward trailing in the same slow fashion

Without one trace of art or touch of passion.

Not dexterous at undoing party ties,

Not easily swayed to break with old allies;

No Derby, now a Whig and now a Tory;

No fine Sir Robert ratting from vain-glory;

No wavering child of fear, like good Trevelyan,

Clinging behind his Nurse upon a pillion;

No shrill Carnarvon, sure to bolt and start,

Being all things "from the bottom of his
    heart;"

No Granville smiling off his country's honour

With every gem her bleeding heroes won her.

Against the old smooth-tongued Flatterer triply
    mailed,

Steadfast when many a trusted spirit failed,

Content to wait for power or to forego,

He stands unmoved whatever whirlwinds blow.

The cheers for Hartington had scarce subsided

When forward to the footlights Goschen glided.

How oft in England men of alien race·

Seek more her honour, blush at her disgrace,

Delight her splendours more to glorify

Than the true children of her own grey sky !

Lives there a stouter champion of her fame

Than German Goschen with his Jewish name?

Not England's Israelite Ben Disraeli

Extolled her more than this Rhinelander's son.

Why, Britons, must enthusiasms repel ye?

Is not your coldness rather overdone?

Most welcome after Hartington's chill platitudes

Were Goschen's heat and even Goschen's attitudes ;

Yes, having fed on ices to satiety,

Some cherry-brandy was a warm variety.

" Great " is a word too often misapplied

And must by me to Goschen be denied;

But many things not small are still not great,

And Goschen is a bulwark of the State.

A keen clear mind, a tongue epigrammatic,

A man of fire amid a race phlegmatic;

Strong in defence, determined in assault,

On Error's trail not often found at fault;

Half Liberal and half Conservative,

Content alone in just the mean to live.

To make a sort of semi-Coalition

It seemed an unavoidable condition

Some Whig must at the Tory Council sit.

What statesman for the hybrid seat were fit?

'T is said that every bullet finds its billet;

The seat is empty—Goschen, then, will fill it.

Uprose, when Goschen sat, that man of pith

The right Right Honourable Mr. Smith,

Whose fate it seems (however fair his dream is)

A Commoner to linger *in extremis,*

And never be, it matters not who else is,

Apotheosized quite and *in excelsis ;*

But who, whatever sphere his soul inherits,

Will always be a man of many merits.

Too full of homely useful common-sense

To clothe a single thought in eloquence,

Welcome relief from Gladstonism and Dizziness,

Straightforward, truthful, honest man of business,

Plain English of the plainest English order,

Incapable of crossing Reason's border.

(Seeing distinctly just their noses' length,

They take weak sight for intellectual strength,

And poetry is folly, they agree,

Because it tells of things they cannot see.)—

Successor to the Churchills and Hicks-Beaches,

Better thy silence oft than half their speeches ! . .

But there goes he whom certain seasons back

The unworthier Irish nicknamed " Foxy Jack."

Yes, they had learned to fear his resolute sway.

And cowering at his foot rebellion lay.

I saw him oft in Dublin, riding by

With anxious face, but ever-fearless eye,

When on the unscathed assassin's weapon yet

The blood of Burke and Cavendish was wet,

When every hedgerow bore a crimson stain,

And murder lurked in every street and lane.

Erect he rode amid the sullen crowd,

Sad, careworn, sick, yet self-possessed and proud,

An English noble undismayed by death,

Fit to have served the Great Elizabeth.

He grappled with a dark invisible foe,

He dragged him from his lair, he laid him low ;

A true-born soldier trained in Nature's school,

A true-born king, men said, foreframed for rule.

But who could dream that he who ruled to-day

To-morrow would his sceptre cast away,

The pilot who had saved the ship from wreck

Would cut its cables when he 'd left its deck ?

What wrought the change in Spencer ?   Can it be,

Unnerved at last, he sought his brain to free

From the dread vision of the murderer's knife,

And sighed for pleasures of a peaceful life ?

Or deemed he that no arm except his own

Could wield the sword that kept rebellion down,—

That, he being gone, remained no better shift

Than let the ungovernable country drift ?

Was it his own or other men's exertion

That brought about that singular " conversion ? "

Nay, was it but the Old Magician's wiles,

The tongue persuasive, the bewitching smiles,

The wand of Hawarden that with one light wave

Transformed him from a master to a slave ? . .

To Erin's Isle I do not mean to roam,

Because I seek a *thorough* change from home ;

But, though I 've shirked that land of saints and

      caitiffs,

I 've not escaped its patriotic natives ;

And therefore with its grievances (as painted

By Irish brushes) I am well acquainted.

I met what might have been an Irish Member

Travelling by Kew to London in the train,

In whom I recognized a burning ember

Of fierce rebellion trampled on in vain.

Assuming that I was his country's foe,

And out my brains his blunderbuss must blow,

He set himself before me and most shrilly

Began to talk of Ireland willy-nilly.

" Do you deny that we 're a race opprest ? "—

" Believe me, nothing 's farther from my breast ! "—

" Yes, sir, you do, and by the seat I sit on,

I tell you, you 're a base and bloody Briton."—

" Excuse me, sir, your language grows so hot "—

" Insult me, and I 'll shoot you on the spot ! "—

"To insult you I respectfully decline, sir."—

" Then you 're a coward, and can only whine, sir."—

" You 're welcome, most pugnacious Irishman,"

I said and smiled, " to kill me, *if you can.*"

At this he cooled, and asked my frank opinion

Of Ireland under England's proud dominion.

And thus I answered :—"Sir, I know your Island

By many men is held a very vile land,

Much over-peopled by a hybrid race

That can 't abide in peace in any place,

Vindictive and irascible and shifty,

Uncleanly and untruthful and unthrifty,

That hug their hate as others hug their love,

Or only nurse the loves their hates approve—

Look in your glass and you will comprehend me—

(From men with restless eyeballs Lord defend me !);

And yet with glimmerings of attractive light,

Like meteors breaking from the gloom of night,—

An inconvenient show of virtuous phases

That stupid English judgments much amazes,

A jack-o'-lantern lustre that deceives them

And lures them into quagmires, and there leaves
     them.

Sir, that 's too sweeping.   'T is your noisy few

That make your Island hateful to the view.

No kindlier race upon this planet dwells

Than that which haunts the Wicklow hills and
      dells ;

No worthier folk inhabit field or town

Than they who brighten happy, smiling Down ;

Ay, and kind Irish hearts there are, and merry,

Even amid the blood-stained glens of Kerry.

'T is such as you, sir, work your Isle's disgrace,

By deeds, by words, mean, dastardly, and base.

You perpetrate your crimes and ne'er relent,

And " persecution " call your punishment,

Name equity "injustice " if it thwart

The wishes of your harmless little heart,

And when you 've picked men's pockets, and they 've
      smit you,

Cry out that they are cruel to have hit you.

O sir, if I were England, let me tell you,

To Russia, Prussia, France, I 'd gladly sell you,

To rid my soul of all the botheration

And endless talk about an Irish " nation."

But were I England, this could never be

If I would still be Mistress of the Sea ;

For what must be your happy Home Rule's
    ending ?

More men and ships for England's coast-defending ;

New dangers in each European broil ;

A Russian fleet at Cork, a French in Foyle.

Nay, were I England, I should have to clasp

Your Island tight and tighter in my grasp ;

So, then, my furnace I should pile more fire on,

And rule your country with a rod of iron.

But England I am not, and I perceive

The Siren doth her dainty nets enweave

Most dexterously round the Saxons' hearts,

And yet may gain her ends by woman's arts.

Hath she not lulled old Merlin in her lap,

And well at Scottish Rosebery set her cap,

Led the strong Spencer by a silken thread,

And found a champion in the stainless Stead,

Among her lovers counted sainted Ripon,

And Morley forced his Christian garb to slip on,

And captive Blunt led captive in her train,

And Aberdeen entangled in her chain?

Sweet Bully Bottom Harcourt now reposes

Between her white arms, garlanded with roses.

And hath not lately too the fair deceiver

Put her *comether* quite on Shaw Lefevre?

And Labouchere, whose name is one with Truth,

And Graham, that inestimable youth,

And Wilfred Lawson, with his wit and water,

Have all the wealth of all their wisdom brought her.

Then she can boast still eighty Members *free*,

Her ever-faithful Parnell and O'Shea,

Town-Councillors from Boyle to Ballyhooley,

Sir Thomas Grattan Esmonde, and Gillooley.

Sir, aided thus, whatever England's need,

The Home Rule brig will certainly succeed—

Nay, every timid foot may now embark on it

Since philanthropic Plimsoll's set his mark on

    it!"

At this with rage he foamed, and drew a knife,

Intent on taking my immortal life.

I parried the fell weapon with my stick,

And out flew sparks electrical and thick.

(He took me then for some distinguished player).

He crossed himself and offered up a prayer,

Turned blue, as if his blood began to freeze,

And all but begged for pardon on his knees.

Just then the engine neared another station

And with a whistle drowned the conversation,

And I, unwilling any more to rile him,

Stopped at the Æsthetes' Lunatic Asylum—

I mean that curious place by Turnham Green,

Where red-tiled houses from the train are seen,

Mild eyes æsthetic to attract and please,

Stuck here and there 'mid blooming apple-trees ;

Where, dressed in garments of a bygone age,

The people act all day as on a stage ;

Where coldness and discomfort are a study,

And windows damned unless their light be muddy ;

Where every box must be unique and old,

And every bedstead crumbling into mould—

One spacious lumber-room wherein are tumbled

The treasures of ten thousand Ghettos jumbled;

Old kettles from the stores of East End brokers,

Old clocks, old cupboards, shovels, fenders, pokers,

Chippendale tables that have lost their legs,

Old silver spoons too frail for breaking eggs,

Worm-eaten chairs of long-forgotten families,

Old pots coeval with the rout at Ramillies,

Old stools perhaps Bubb Dodington has sat on

Or Chesterfield or Lumpkin laid his hat on—

Anything dingy ever used by man,

Or woman, so it savours of Queen Anne.

I walked about the stage with studied grace,

Yet somehow felt most sadly out of place.

The actors saw 't was plainly not my line,

And frowned upon me as a Philistine.

I felt, I must allow, a day too old

To drop into the arch-æsthetic fold ;

Youth is the time for masquerades and folly,

And age for broadcloth and for melancholy ;

So, when I had my little round for fun done,

I left the sacred applegarth for London. . .

Dear ! what a crowd along the railings presses !

I scarce can see the Ride for ladies' dresses.

Alas, while I 've been lost in recollection,

What marvels may have passed without inspection !

Now surely comes a personage amazing,

Else why should all the world be one way gazing ?

Heavens ! who rides by so broad of beam and back,

An elephant upheaved upon a hack ?

What ! is that mass amorphous, ponderous,

That human heap, renowned Historicus ?

He whose prodigious jests by night resound

From Stephen's chaos up to Heaven's profound,

And, having vainly smitten earthly ears

And moved Heaven's angels to unwonted tears,

Roll down, and reaching late our world of woe,

Add one more torture to the damned below?

Is this sublime Silenus of the Law,

This Senatorial Samson and his jaw,

Is this stupendous bulk so broad and bossy

Great England's Lord High Chancellor *in posse*?

O, take him hence! He shadows me with gloom.

His every smile reminds me of the tomb.

O, take him hence! I do not merit this

Extinguishment of all my earthly bliss!

O, take him hence, and let me see no more

The blessed daylight darkened by a bore!

Take back thy champion, Erin, to thy bosom,

And, having found him, see that you do n't lose

    him! . .

Of Radicals I wished to get some notion,

But Chamberlain had gone across the Ocean,

On a hard errand driven by the Fates,—

To patch up treaties with the Yankee States;

And Bright was altogether out of town,

And only sending letters up and down

To various correspondents who might nobble 'im

For counsel on the endless Irish problem ;

And Dilke, whose black eclipse was such a loss
      for us,

Was sipping coffee somewhere on the Bosphorus ;

And Morley, with Lord Ripon, was appearing

In Christian parts at theatres in Erin ;

Trevelyan to be caught was quite too slippery ;

And all the rest are but the merest frippery.

  But heartily I wish that I had seen

And heard John Bright while yet his age is green.

An honest politician is so fair a thing

'T is pity, if there 's one, to miss so rare a thing ;

And, judged, I hold, according to his light,

No man more honest breathes than bluff John
      Bright.

His old " peace policy " has proved, no doubt,

A little weak, as things are turning out.

We must have order and we sigh for peace,

But will the wicked from their troubling cease?

If not, when Turmoil sweet Persuasion stifles,

What's left to use but truncheons, swords, and rifles?

But Christianity and Commerce call

Alike for peace amid this mundane brawl;

The shrewd commercial Christian shrewdly mea-
        sures

What swells his earthly and his heavenly trea-
        sures.

Thus there is reason in that high appeal

For peace amid the wide world's commonweal;

And, sooth, if Earth had such a boon as this is,

The Heavens themselves might envy her her blisses.

Yet, were I mortal 'mid this world of care,

However I might shrink from battle's din,

I'd hold by old Polonius' words:—" Beware

Of entrance to a quarrel, but, being in,

Bear 't that the opposëd may beware of thee,"—

And never underrate mine enemy,—

A fault of Britons, which, the world well knows,

Oft humbles England to her paltriest foes. . .

Leave baby soldiers to their babies'-rattles,

And pay a corps of *men* to fight your battles. . .

On Chamberlain I 've pondered with mixed
  pleasure ;

I think he too is honest—in a measure.

A Radical who likewise is Imperial

Is Radical of very best material.

Somehow I think he wishes England well,

And would not for mere place her honour sell,—

At least not yet, while still he 's no temptation

To play the Gladstone with this patient nation ;

But truly to my inexperienced eye

In him no serious danger seems to lie.

Upon the Irish case he looks as sound

As any man can look on Irish ground,

Which always is so shifty and so boggy

And shrouded in an atmosphere so foggy
That all who tread it seem in wild gyrations
Revolving in a life of transformations ;
And I, until he 's done some patent ill,
Will hold that Chamberlain is honest still. . .

I 'm tired of musing on these politicians
Who deem themselves so great and are so small—
Why, Bismarck, in his mammoth deglutitions,
In one light morsel might devour them all.
A man of letters, were he small or great,
Were now a pleasing thing to contemplate—
And here comes Robert Browning ! . . . I regret
To see the seal of age upon him set.
I saw him last in Florence years ago,
Long ere that massive head was touched with snow,
When Landor's words were truer than to-day,—
An eager watcher looking every way,
A man of buoyant step and grasping eye
That laid its grip on every passer-by,

And read him—not perhaps exactly right,

But always in some interesting light,

And nothing let escape in park or street

Of all that he in rapid walk might meet,

Glancing from Beauty in her chariot down

To the bare foot of beggar or of clown,

From the dull pavement upward to heaven's blue,

And back from heaven again to me or you.

Short, broad, erect, not lithely in his gait,

Unweariable, self-confident, elate,

With easy, drawing-room-educated shoulders—

A presence always cheering to beholders.

To-day, alas ! the largeness of the eye

Is gone, and tamed the fine vivacity,

Less buoyant is the step, the keen-cut brow

More toward its mother-earth begins to bow.

Ay me ! the poets at three-score-and-ten

Cease to be poets and are only men,

And Tennyson and Browning Delphi's god

Hath stamped with mournful letters " Ichabod ! "

Yet hath Sordello lived to hear his claims

To deathless glory sung by girls and dames,

To find that every critic now afraid is

To chide the hoary lion of the ladies,

To sit at ease while Furnivall's Society

Spoon-feeds his large self-love to sick satiety.

Lord ! how this foolish and inconstant world

From folly unto folly still is whirled !

A score of years ago poor Browning's name

Was only whispered with a blush of shame ;

Now I perceive the literary papers

Are following Furnivall's fantastic capers,

And *Athenæum*, *Saturday Review*,

Academy, and eke *Spectator* too,

The Editor most genial and loquacious,

The Editor most graceful and most gracious,

The Editor most liberal though not spacious,

The Editor most kind and most capacious,

All laud his feeblest fancies to the skies,

Declare his darkest devils deities,

And carve upon his pedestal sublime,

" Browning, the Greatest Poet of all Time ! "

Well, this is very well, but after all,

All Editors, down even to ———l

Should, one would think, have sometimes still at
      heart

The interests of literary art,

And not exaggerate in blame or praise

Though they may know exaggeration pays.

And I, who am artistic to the core,

Though liking Browning, cannot but deplore

That the poor public should be led astray,

And taught that Browning writes the proper way,

That verse should be as harsh and rough as shingle,

And Milton's English turned to hobbling jingle,

And men from poesy should nothing gain

But grains of pleasure got with spasms of pain.

  To whatsoever madness critics run

I hold the time's best bard is Tennyson.

Though poorer stuff ne'er dripped from worn-out

    pens

Than *Carmen Seculare* and *The Wrens*,

Though "Go not, happy day" is grievous folly,

And *Harold*'s as insipid as *Queen Molly*,

Though he should ne'er have served us up that

    Supper,

And half his *Idylls* are as dull as Tupper,

Yet he that *In Memoriam* hath writ

High o'er this age's bards enthroned shall sit,

Still reverenced by his country and his Queen,

A Laureate crowned with laurels ever green.

He is no caterer for the sensual herd

Whose pulses nothing noble ever stirred;

No manufacturer of amorous ditties

Inspired amid the smoke and gas of cities;

No Cockney lyrist of the street and square

Who hardly knows a harrier from a hare,

And moulds and mixes mediæval ballads

As cooks concoct their sauces and their salads;

No trickster toadying pressmen for critiques ;

No hanger-on of literary cliques ;

No charlatan with intellectual puzzles

Perplexing the dazed reader Fashion muzzles ;

But one of Nature's poets, mingling heart

Still with the music of elaborate art,

From Nature drawing all the sweets he brings us,

And still exalting by the songs he sings us.

This is involuntary admiration ;

He merits not my *moral* approbation.

Far better to my liking are the inborn

Rare virtues of the smaller poet Swinburne.

He was my willing servant for a time,

And somewhat prostituted English rhyme

To doubtful uses, and with sensual spice

Spoilt critic-palates, never over-nice,

So that the pure Castalian springs no more

They care to taste, nor heed though they should

      pour

In clear glad music and refreshful song

Down from the Delphian hollows all day long.

One says, " There was a little craft in this

Betrayal of the Muses with a kiss,—

A stroke of business in this best of ages

When half each book is advertising pages.

A bombshell of unseemly fancies hurled

Into its midst might rouse the listless world,

And make the hurler famous in a day,

Where modest bards are left to fade away.

This is an age when men attract attention

By doing things that some would blush to mention,

Then, having wallowed well in sloughs of shame,

Walk evermore serene the halls of Fame,

Become 'respectable,'—the people's leaders,

Great in the Senate, loved of lady readers ;

Demoralize at first, and then instruct,

And claim of Virtue's self the usufruct.

So Bradlaugh, having horrified Society,

Begins to pose, a preacher of propriety ;

And Chastelard, self-cured of ribald rabies,

Betakes himself to writing Odes to Babies."—. .

But no ! O'er all ambition's mean devices

The soul of *Atalanta*'s bard arises ;

And he is still a poet and a true one,

Though milder now than when he was a new one ;

To whom, in scribbling (when I knew no better),

Myself in some degree have been a debtor,

Which freely I acknowledge, while repenting

Things rhythmic done without my will's consenting.

I saw poor Chastelard some time ago

Down somewhere toward the Seven Dials go.

He paused to peer into a printer's shop.

He looked autumnal, rather, at the top.

I touched him on the shoulder, and he started ;

He claspt my hand—then swift away he darted,

And down a lane the little poet ran on,

Followed at heel and pelted by Buchanan.

These Three the critics in the public sight

The foremost places yield.   Perhaps they 're right.

Morris, the "Singer of an empty Day,"

Has seldom soothed *me* with his jolting lay.

He told a story well ; could wield his pencil,

And graphic pictures drew with that utensil ;

But something always seemed a little wrong

About his paces as he jigged along.

(His Muse is dead.   The socialist upholsterer

Will hardly with anarchic ballads bolster her.)

That nursery-Dante, Morris of the *Hades,*

Is harmless reading for insipid ladies ;

The mild musician, with his silver medal,

Still plays his harpsichord with broken pedal,

And calls the toneless instrument his "harp ; "

And still he 'll play for folk that are not sharp

To notice that his melodies are tuneless,

His day-songs sunless and his nocturnes moonless.

Arnold—I mean Sir Edwin—must confess

He owes much to his brethren of the Press ;

And Arnold—I mean Matthew Arnold—owes

No more to modest verse than polished prose.

Amid the bowl of bards I might have tossed in

An Austin Dobson or an Alfred Austin;

Buchanan these might join, to sink or swim,

And one or two whose lustre's not more dim;

But this my cup of riches soon would drain,

And if I pour the lees out, what remain?

For who would noble Poesy degrade

By calling poets those whose dismal trade

Is forging verses void of thought and passion

(I wish some Jeffrey these would lay his lash on),

Those cliques of small persistent poetasters

Who of the trick of rime are would-be masters,

But never yet, for all their toil and dole,

Have touched the springs of any human soul;

Who, though their rhythmic "lilt" correct and
       terse is,

Have never got past writing "nonsense-verses";

Who love the poet's *name*, and purr, and paw it,

But would not know a poem if they saw it?

What man who Milton, Shakespeare, Byron loves,

Whom Dante, Goethe, Wordsworth, Shelley moves,

Could read without a smile their dusty stuff

That every petty critic's learnt to puff?

Deluded by the weekly weak Reviews,

Whose whims our wiser Britons but amuse,

The honest Yankees now their praises shower

On these presumptuous froth-flies of an hour.

God help thee, Poesy, if men conceive thee

As nothing better than these nothings leave thee. . .

Still harping on the poets? Well, I know it.

The noblest work of Heaven's a true-born poet.

They fascinate, but yet disturb my bliss,

So once for all let me the tribe dismiss.

Of all the bards I know my say is said.

The works of Armstrong I have never read. . .

What, my good fellow! Are you not aware

That I have paid already for the chair? . .

A penny? . . Though my fortunes are decaying,

Excellent sir, I yet will go on paying

Penny on penny, so you'll keep away

And let me feel heaven's breezes while I may.

And yet I do n't see why I *should* pay *twice*. . .

Do n't beg my pardon. Sir, you 're much too nice! . .

Ha! ha! . . The righteous rascal! How respectable! . .

These English really are a race delectable.

They cheat and sin with such unruffled calm

That every wolf among them looks a lamb—

Ay, search the earth "from China to Peru,"

No scoundrel, English scoundrel, equals you! . .

How strange that none of all these million eyes

Has happened yet my form to recognize

In this my nineteenth-century disguise!

Some dimly note in passing, little caring,

Something distinguished, doubtless, in my bearing;

Some antiquated spinsters eye me queerly,

But that, no doubt, is maiden coyness merely;

Some country parsons take me for His Grace

Of York, or that Great Statesman out of place,

Or Lincoln's Bishop (vinegar and nitre!)

Compelled in Town to go without his mitre;

Some tinted ladies smile at me so boldly

I'm forced to recompense their glances coldly;

They seem to take me for a titled rip,

And go about to get me in their grip;

Some giddy girls, whose morals and whose fancies

Alike are nursed on yellow-backed romances,

Perceive a something in me devilish,

And flirting with the Devil is their wish;

Some take me for an actor off the boards,

And some a novice of the House of Lords;

But, as I still am modest and discreet,

I'm not much noticed yet in park or street.

I sat hobnobbing with invisible Sin

One Sunday in a Cambridge country-inn

While other (better) folk were on their knees,

When in a party trooped in twos and threes,

A-dust with trudging many a country road,

Led by a broad-built man who stoutly strode,

Grey-eyed, grey-bearded, and with dusty curls.

They looked Bohemians, and they spoke like
      churls,

But learned terms were mingled with their talk,

And learning seemed to dog them in their walk—

Indeed they could not call for beer and cheese

Except in symbols of the Sciences.

I thought it sport to watch them from afar,

So crossed my legs and lighted a cigar.

Silent they ate—it seems a Cambridge way

To be as gruff and graceless as you may—

Till one who looked less English than the rest,

A dark man in a velvet tunic dressed,

Blithe, flexile, and with mirth in either eye,

With some bright sally woke the company ;

And then there followed a disjointed chat

On many topics, while I, listening, sat.

They rose to speculation's loftiest level,

And settled down at last upon the Devil—

I hid myself amid a cloud of smoke,

And bent an ear to each one as he spoke.

An orange-tawny-bearded man with glasses,

Who spake unmoved as monumental brasses,

With clenchëd teeth and face that looked one sneer

Of discontent and inward suffering drear,

A constant agonizing inanition

Of ravenous and insatiable ambition

(Or so to me appeared it—but I gauge

All men perhaps by mine own inward rage),

Gathered himself together, stern as Fate,

And in harsh accents thus addressed his plate :—

" The Devil served his purpose well enough

When barbarous Ignorance battened on such stuff;

But now he 's left no place wherein to dwell

Since Modern Science has abolished Hell."

Whereat those laughed who were for laughter able,

And I drew in my feet beneath the table.

The grey man, who his pipe had meanwhile lighted,

Smiled not, but smoked as if the jest he slighted;

Then muttered drily, " Modern Science boasts

It has abolished too the Lord of Hosts."

" The House of Lords, no doubt, will follow next,"

Said one who straightway blushed and looked

      perplext.

(What though the others failed its point to see,

I liked this speaker's covert irony.)

Then one, who was a politician clearly,

And thought of governing (but not too dearly),

Suggested, " For the ignorant and the fool,

For women, and for children still at school,

The Devil is a useful institution,

Serving as a deterrent from pollution,

Perhaps preventing even revolution,

And for State purposes the worn-out fogy

Might still be kept together as a bogy !"—

Naught hurts my feelings like an idiot's sneers.

I felt the blood rush tingling to my ears.

I flashed a look of anger at the creature—

He only thought I must be some lay-preacher.

(The self-sufficient man is always blind,

And sees not what's before him or behind).

The fool at his own fooling joined the laugh,

And called, with pomp, for some more shandy-gaff.

Then like a gust of wind they rose and passed

Quickly, as if each moment were their last,

Striding away in agonizing walk;

And, left alone, I mused upon their talk.

" The world," thought I,—" I say it not in grief—

Is simply perishing of unbelief.

Men that can't see their noses save with glasses

Presume to solve what human sight surpasses;

Even Science, that at best but dimly sees,

Will dogmatize about the Mysteries.

'T is this that makes it easy, for my mirth,

To move about unnoticed o'er the Earth,

And, laughing at each Solomon I meet,

To play the Devil with his self-conceit." . .

Nay, I am Evil, I am Anarchy,

I am Confusion—have ye conquered *me* ? . .

There goes a Bishop ! . . . Yes, that shovel-hat

Would guide me, were he ne'er so sleek and fat.

Stanley I 've heard, and Jowett, in my time,

Describe a Church ideal and sublime.

Among the cleric ranks—I must allow it—

There 's not a broader mind than that of Jowett.

Stanley's was wide, but Jowett's still is wider,—

So wide that out of sight there Truth might hide

      her ;

I do n't know what it holds, or what it does not,

And of its secrets that I know, I 'll buzz not.

In the grey Abbey oft I 've heard him preach,

And much approved what he 's assayed to teach—

A Church with all the elements of schism

Within it like the colours in a prism,

Though breaking up what Light it doth enrol,

Still, like the prism, one unbroken whole—

A Church, in fact, was to mine eye presented

From all whose doctrines all her sons dissented,

Just brooked because men's freaks it would not
     fetter,

And subsidized by State for want of better ;

A Church that reckoned as her faithful sheep

Whatever cared within her pale to creep,—

Wolves, bears, or jackals, lions, tigers, hogs,

Panthers, or hinds, or ladies' collie-dogs,

Frequenters of conventicles suburban,

Or any chutney-merchant in a turban,

The British Buddhist or the true Chinese,

The Zulus or the feathered Cherokees,

The ritualistic curate slight and sleek,

The Jew, the Turk, the Gallican, the Greek,

The man whose god is Gothic Art or Norman,

The wifeless priest or patriarchal Mormon ;—

A Church whose very basis of existence

Were yielding to dissent without resistance,

Where every wight should worship as it pleased him,

Or worship nothing if the humour seized him,

And all should by their deeds and words admit

That Truth's attainment passes human wit.

Now, still there may remain an English Church

Till pious William grips it as a perch

To flutter up to power and place once more,

Striking it down in wild attempts to soar;

And every year and month to me it seems

Assuming more the shape of Jowett's dreams.

Yes, Divine Service I have much attended

As up and down through English land I 've
    wended,

And fifty petty churches seem to-day

Sprung fungus-like from one in its decay,—

Broad, High, Low, High-Broad, Low-Broad, High-
    and-Dry,

Broad-Ritualistic, Ritualistic-High,

Dry-Low, or Evangelical-Hysterical,

Half-Plym., Whole-Slim, All-Square, and Semi-
    Spherical,

Church-scouting-Everlasting-Punishment,

Church-holding-Hell-Heaven's-highest-ornament,

Church-Calvinistic, Church-distinct-Arminian,

Church-Arian, Church-Agnostic, Church-Socinian,

Church-looking-on-Religion-as-a-slow-thing,

Church-everything-you-like, or simply no thing;

A chaos of all sorts of contradictories

Unreconciled by logic's nicest victories.

Now all these churchlets, from one faint Church

    sprouting,

Each little shadowy cult the others flouting,

What are they but a sickly suppuration

Of Faith becoming morbid through prostration?

Which things to me, an old observer, point

To something in this kingdom out of joint.

Can Morals flourish where Religion dies?

What shall uplift the mortal to the skies?

Religion grown a luxury or whim

Which each man alters as it pleases *him*,

A thing to number with the "fads" and follies

And puppets infants dandle with their dollies,

Whatever compromising minds may plan,

Can work no miracle in bestial man.

And yet this Church a kind of sanction yields

Still to the State that still its being shields;

Still throws the mantle of respectability

O'er morals, makes its service seem gentility;

Encourages a social regularity;

Teaches decorum; organizes charity;

Ay, even in suspended animation,

Is worth preserving by this mighty nation;

For none can tell, when Faith is on the wane,

What touch may wake her into life again.

Meanwhile, I, Satan, drink to its confusion,

To all its votaries daily new delusion,

To Lincoln lasting strength, and health to Jowett,

Power to each hand that earthward helps to
      bow it,

And force to Gladstone's axe that never fails

Uplifted now to strike its life from Wales! . .

My Lords and gentlemen, "The Church!" . .

Ta-ta ! . .

Ha ! ha ! ha ! ha ! ha ! ha ! ha ! ha ! ha ! ha ! . .

I weigh with those who make this Church their
home
The men who from it headlong run to Rome.
When to believe in nothing most are driven,
These in believing all things find their heaven.
Credulity and weakness both are human,
Yet neither surely taints the breast of Newman.
To rise to power most men are ever planning,
But who can prove ambition governs Manning?
What wild confusion of the wistful heart
Made such from creed to creed impetuous dart,
What panic of the Spirit o'er them came
That, in sheer frenzy, plunged them into flame? . .

Close by the pulpit in a chapel small
I sat to hear an English Cardinal.

Not like a foe I went, in rude invasion,

But simple, childlike, open to persuasion.

His eye, that seemed to look in all men's eyes,

Caught mine amid the rest without surprise ;

But when he saw my eagerness for light,

He gave me all his rede with all his might.

An eager, keen, lean face, without one ray

Of joy or rapture in its ashen grey ;

An eye that, half suspicious, half defiant,

Seems loveless, lustreless, and uncompliant ;

A litheness of the body and the mind

That makes the man within them hard to find ;

A voice incisive ; an incisive finger

That lights on sores, but nowhere loves to linger ;

Some temper 'mid a studious calm betraying ;

Some subtle shuffling of the cards in playing ;

Some yielding to unfairness toward a foe

In resolute straining for his overthrow ;

In language careful, measured, mathematical ;

In faith adopted almost full fanatical ;

Not swaying with the enthusiast's warmth and
    boldness,
But penetrating with an east wind's coldness;
Clear with the gleam and glassiness of ice,
And liberal in logical device.
If but his premises I could have granted,
My creed I should most surely have recanted. . .

I have not much affection for the Law,
So of the Men of Wigs I little saw—
At least in recent wanderings up and down
Among the doubtful places of the town.
The Church, although it fancies it eludes me,
Oft folds me to its heart.   The Law excludes me.
Law, based on Faith, enforced where evil lurks,
Is death upon the Devil and his works;
And English law, though now and then it blunders,
Sounds in mine ears like Heaven's eternal thunders.
Of Barrister and Judge I've nought to say.
I think they do their work from day to day,

Whatever motive actuates the breast,

Respectably, while feathering each his nest ;

And, tolerant as I am of peccadillos,

I think they may recline upon their pillows

As peacefully as some of sacred station

Or any statesman who has " found salvation."

And, though there may be Judges too with flaws,

How ably all expound their country's laws !

I hardly can recount the brilliant names.

There 's Herschell, Bramwell, and there will be
      James ;

There 's Selborne—or there *was ;* there 's High-
      Church Coleridge,

Fit to plough up false logic by the whole ridge ;

There 's Butt, who uses all a mortal's forces

(And needs them) to decide the world's divorces ;

There 's . . . really I forbear to think them over.

I envy all.   Though none quite live in clover,

They 're happier here than in that Isle of Slaughters,

Out, where the sun sets, there, across the Waters. . .

What's he, now, with the eye-glass in his eye,

Perched on the four-in-hand that's passing by?

An actor? Can an actor sit so high?

Yes, yes, I've seen the same that now I scan

Act also on the boards the gentleman—

Indeed he looked (I can't imagine how)

A good deal less the actor then than now.

I like the craft, have acted much myself,

And have not yet been laid upon the shelf;

And nothing would I think or say severe

Of actors that might hurt them should they hear.

But they themselves must think it rather curious,

When acted plays are paltry things and spurious,

When England's Drama stultifies the land,

That actors on a pinnacle should stand.

Yes, in the Drama's palmiest days, we know,

Despised they lived, their art was rated "low;"

Now, when the Drama is a thing so base,

The world enfolds them in its fond embrace

(At least the lady-players it caresses),

And Royalty itself the boxes blesses.

You dine the players, ask them to your suppers,

Lend them your hacks, your saddles, and your
      cruppers,

Invite them to your country-seats for sport,

Smile at their weddings, usher them to Court,

Purchase their portraits, treasure up their busts,

Make them dispensers of your children's trusts,

Nay, envy them the very boards they walk on,

And seek the Stage yourselves to rant and talk on,

Rear mimic theatres in private houses,

Or act your pastorals where the heifer browses,

Ay, all but set the Stage o'er Mother Church,

And meanwhile leave the Drama in the lurch.

    The Drama is old England's brightest glory,

Her loftiest feat in literary story.

Each traveller a spectator's sure to be at her

Finest performance in her foremost theatre—

"That's the Lyceum," I was told, and so

To the Lyceum I was bound to go.

I went, and saw Myself (with sundry thrills)

Caricatured by Irving and by Wills.

'T is clear there is no reverence in this age

Felt for the Devil on or off the Stage.

Goethe, though treating me not wholly well,

Remembered the Archangel ere he fell;

But Wills and Irving vulgarize my part,

And mere scene-shifting strangles Goethe's art.

Outraged I sat.   I could not choose but frown

At that lean Devil skipping up and down,

At travesties of Goethe's lordly rime

Mixed with tomfooleries of the Pantomime.

Think of the glories of Elizabeth !

Say, is not *this* the Drama's lingering death ?

Garrick compare, his Shakespeare's tragic sock on,

With Irving kissing monkeys on the Brocken !

Yet Irving 's scarce to blame.   If all the Nation

Delight to watch him in that situation,

To see their ablest actor play the fool

And sink in Tragedy to rival Toole,

Why should he starve his purse or waste his wit

By playing *Hamlet* to an empty pit?

Why not keep climbing still the Brocken's heights,

And kissing apes, for ten more thousand nights?

It is the world's fault if your art is bad;

Art follows public taste or sane or mad.

The English-speaking public vaster grows,

And all must see the latest London shows;

No spectacle must ever be withdrawn

Till all the population 's come and gone;

Then, when the folk at home have ceased to laud it,

Remains that all America applaud it;

And so the same false art from shore to shore

Moves round the earth until it pays no more.

I 've gone about by gaslight to and fro

To theatres from Kensington to Bow;

The inside and the outside have inspected;

A member of the * * * * * * been elected;

With Negroes danced (in dances quite informal)

On frosty days to keep my blood-heat normal;

And when, at night, the longest play was over,

Supped at the * * * * * * * like a midnight rover;

With actors over wine have cracked a filbert,

Talking of Hebrew Sullivan and Gilbert;

Seen Ellen Terry in her Doctor's dress,

And mourned with her in Gretchen's dire distress;

Heard Beerbohm Tree to Bernard-Beere once sigh
      on knee,

And worshipped Anderson in fair Hermionè;

Laughed till my sides have ached at Thorne and
      Toole,

And under Hermann Vezin gone to school;

From melancholy musings grown too merry

In looking at the face of Edward Terry;

Felt passionate Eastlake all my senses daze,

And wept with Barrett at his latest plays;

And, after days of weariness, to end all,

Sat happy, watching charming Mrs. Kendal;

And all I have to say of England's stage is,

Its tale is writ in bygone history's pages.

Brilliant and many talents on it shine;

Of comic actors England is a mine;

But poetry from Britain's stage has faded;

For noble art men's minds are all too jaded;

Shakespeare himself, if living in these days,

Would leave Augustus Harris to write plays,

Would let the critics about roundels rave on,

And fatten sheep at Stratford-upon-Avon. . .

But pause, my brain! Might not this stage-
distraction,

Before there comes a still more mad reaction,

Yet lead the public taste to fairer ways,

And bring again the Drama's halcyon-days?

Then, when the people yearned for loftier art,

Some mightier poet from the gloom might start,

Some Shakespeare dealing with the deeds sublime

And vaster knowledge of the later time,

To rouse, to help, to chasten, to entrance,

With dreams divine and gorgeous circumstance! . .

Pshaw! . . What Utopian vision blinds mine eye! . .

Enough.   The Drama's dying.   Let it die. . .

The English Novel too, it seems agreed,

Like many English things, has run to seed.

Who wears the mantle now of Dickens, pray?

Where is the genius of a Thackeray?

Where the fine power of Lytton when he drew

Rienzi underneath the Italian blue?

In worthy Wilkie Collins must we seek

A Trollope, though poor Trollope was but weak?

Is Black or Blackmore worthy to unloose

The latchet of immortal Eliot's shoes?

Who hears an echo now of all the cant

About John Shorthouse and *John Inglesant?*

Behind the times I'm far too great a laggard

To kneel to Payn, Besànt, or Rider Haggard;

The innumerable horrors of Miss Braddon

Might suit the taste of Moloch or Abaddon,

But, for myself, however dark my *mind*,

I hope my *palate* still may be refined.

As to the rest, in truth I have not read them.

I really cannot open them.   I dread them. . .

But peace !   What " noticeable man " comes by,

Who sees nor dog nor horse nor earth nor sky,

Wandering amid the concourse unaware,

With drooping lips that seem to move in prayer ;

Tall ; pale ; his face in sad appeal upraised ;

Intent on nothing outward ; calm, yet dazed ;

With arm uplifted and its hand suspended,

As if to drop an alms it were extended ?

Quaint picture for the Devil's contemplation—

Historic Lecky lost in meditation !

I read his gentle histories now and then

When I am weary in my fiery den ;

He cools my lips and tenderly bedews 'em

Like Lazarus come from Father Abraham's bosom ;

He soothes my troubled mind with tranquil story
Told softly with no straining after glory;
Sweet, temperate, impartial, conscientious,
Not pompous, or disjointed, or sententious;
Not eager, like the late-lost gifted Green,
Who paints as one red sunset every scene;
Not saying things aggressive and unpleasant,
Like Freeman, with the brusqueness of a peasant—
Freeman the foe of Kingsley, now a tool
Of hot-brained faction clamouring for Home
          Rule;
Not dealing in the startling and surprising,
Like Seeley, brass in beater's-leaf disguising;
Not bungling in his very happiest mood,
And doomed to bungle still, like luckless Froude—
Poor Froude who made the Irish hate him so
By telling what they did not wish to know,
And telling it without the tact that kills
Ill-flavoured truth's harsh taste as jam the pill's;
No quack historian with his syllabubs;

Surpassed in breadth and strength by only
    Stubbs. . .

I heard an Irish critic named O'Brawley

Declare he was the "Irish Lord Macaulay."

If "Irish" means serene and equable,

That epithet might fit him passing well.

But what poor praise Irish from Irish meet!

Can nothing Irish stand on its own feet?

Must Connemara be "the Irish *Highlands*,"

Wild Arran only "Irish *Western Islands*,"

Killarney just "the Irish *Tay* or *Leven*,"

And loveliest Wicklow but "the Irish *Devon?*"

Say Goldsmith, then, but flaunts in *Johnson's*
    socks,

And Edmund Burke declare "the Irish *Fox!*"

Nay, Irish things in Irish raiment deck ye.

Let Irish Lecky be "the Irish Lecky. . ."

I say, this mild historian soothes my soul,

And yet he's done me damage on the whole.

His *European Morals* and his *Rationalism*

Disturb me like his Anti-Irish-Nationalism—

Yes, 'mid the turmoil of our stormy weather

They fret me like the tickling of a feather.

He certainly has dealt a hurtful blow

At that fast-melting Home Rule Man-of-Snow,

And, after Stephen's giant club's assay,

Has helped, with Froude, to shovel him away.

But yet this overthrow I scarce lament—

There always must be Irish discontent;

And if through Lecky poor Religion gains

One convert, she may take him for her pains. . .

What! Millais? Leighton? . . 'T is a sight to
    charm—

Apollo and Adonis arm-in-arm ! . .

The wordless arts, that do n't assail the ear,

Amid this world of noise to me are dear,

And very pleasant to my weary sight

A passing vision of their men of might. . .

But hang it ! Wherefore should they look at *me*

With such a close and puzzled scrutiny? . .

Yes, gentlemen, I much admire you both,

But to be stared at I am something loath.

I thought I looked quite sleek and commonplace.

What, pray, can ye decipher in my face? . .

'T is but their painters' study—so, no matter.

They care but for the outside of the platter.

They paint the lights and tints of hair and skin,

But seldom show without the man within.

To paint the Soul 's beyond your art's ambitions,

Ye two most famous Royal Academicians!

But then we 've learnt that men have now no souls

(*Vide* the *Nineteenth Century* of Knowles),

And so ye can't be blamed if ye omit it,

And paint the Body that was made to fit it. . .

To Piccadilly's Gallery I turned in—

The rooms great England's artist-genius burned in.

A chaos of wild paint on endless walls,

Saints, poultry, portraits, sea-views, waterfalls,

A blinding blaze of wood, street, sky, storms, lake—

One gazes at it till the eyeballs ache,

Squeezed by stout ladies, elbowed by stout men,

Pressed, packed, and poked, like cattle in a pen,

Tangled in flounces, trodden on with boots

By boors that beg your pardon when it suits,

Driven sideways from the point at which you aim,

And *out*, in sick confusion, blind and lame—

Unless you go there when the world 's in bed,

And then it 's empty as an æsthete's head.

Then to that sanctuary of Art's high priests,

The Grosvenor, to taste ambrosial feasts,

I hurried, eager to behold the pictures

Proved great by earning Academic strictures,

Or paintings which their painters deemed too fine

To set before Earth's ordinary swine.

And there I found no crowd, but ample space—

The world forgot that there was such a place.

And from the Grosvenor up and down I went

From gallery to gallery, intent

On satisfying my religious feeling

By means of Art, without the pain of kneeling—

On feeding the deep spiritual emotions

With *paint*, according to the newest notions ;

Till, having stood and gazed in almost all

(A shower of rain had now begun to fall),

My soul found peace where these sweet words were

      seen :—

" Arrangement by one Whistler, here, in Green."

   It was in Bond Street, and the rain was spitting.

To enter in and rest was most befitting—

And pity 't was no chair was there for sitting.

A servitor in green my shilling took,

And in my hand he placed a greenish book,

And through a curtain green I passed, and found

Myself within a room, green, green all round,

Hung with green pictures all in frames of green,

Pale green, grass-green, pea-green, and green of

      bean.

Green were the pictures in their greeny frames,

Green skies, green seas, green coals, and greener
flames,

Green moons, and sunsets green, and green sea-
fishes,

And medleys of green plates and cakes and dishes,

Green men with legs of superhuman thickness,

And green girls dead, or dying, of green-sickness—

Or what seemed girls and men and cups and
cakes

And moons and suns, but might be ducks and
drakes,

Or anything you please ; for, as for drawing,

That was beneath the godlike painter's pawing—

Just as it is beneath your bards of light

To put one word of sense in what they write.

"O Art, Art, Art," I cried, "I feel indeed

Thou satisfiest my spiritual need !

Farewell all dreams of Heaven, all childish cults !

This is the true Religion—for adults !" . .

Fools ! .. Art, to gratify the Spirit's yearning,

Itself must from the Spirit's yearning spring.

With all their marvellous skill, *technique,* and
      learning,

Your modern artists paint no noble thing.

Your fault again, O misbelieving World,

Not theirs, whose finer energies are furled,

Or hang as dead, amid the lifeless air,

But might like crowded sails o'er gorgeous seas

Waft them sublime, if ye but gave the breeze.

What might not Millais, Leighton, Poynter paint

If not quite crippled by your base constraint ?

Splendid the genius and the skill to-day

That England owns, but England's sons betray.

Painters, like actors, bend to social need—

They follow downward as the vulgar lead.

Delicate Leighton, fine and finer grown,

Paints merely flesh, omitting brawn and bone ;

And Stone and Millais (doubtless unawares)

Turn advertisers of the soaps of Pears !

Most lovely are the visions of their minds,
And richer gifts my searching nowhere finds;
But public whims from loftiest flights deter—
They bow to Liverpool and Manchester,
And bloated cotton-lords and city zeros
Usurp the canvas meant for gods and heroes. . .

If I were man, I can't believe but I
Should greatly mourn o'er man's mortality.
Decay and Death, how dismal and how drear!
How horrible man's losses year by year!
How horrible to see each living face
Lose all its beauty, every form its grace!
To see the mind that swayed you with its might
Grow feebler, languishing with mortal blight,
Till all that you have striven with tears to save
Drops down at last into a loathsome grave! . .
These melancholy thoughts arise, no doubt,
From seeing intellectual lights go out
So often lately when I least expected

And where mine eyes for guidance were directed.

There was dear Ruskin.   Where could any find

Upon the crust of Earth a fairer mind?

His was a force that stirred the dullest heart

With love of Nature, and, through Nature, Art;

A lovely mind with shapes of beauty haunted,

Through which Thought moved as through a realm

    enchanted.

I saw him first beneath those snowy heights

He hath illumined with such magic lights,

I thought to find their beauty in his face

Reflected with an archangelic grace.

Not so.   On Leman's Lake of skyey blue

He came aboard a steamboat off Montreux.

He gazed upon the waters, and a sneer

Spread o'er his face, methought, from ear to ear;

He gazed upon the mountains, and it seemed

As if of Whistler's pots of paint he dreamed;

He gazed upon the blue unclouded skies,

And seemed to groan within, and shut his eyes.

This disappointed me ; but even then
He was a seraph in this world of men.
But now, Art's hierarch, great Nature's priest,
What is he but a piteous sight and *triste ?*
Preacher of queer, fantastic, meaningless,
Dull dogmas, softening to his own caress,
God of a self-built temple, he is found,
His worshippers extended on the ground,
Fed with the fruits of vanity o'erblown,
By no heart.so adored as by his own.

These are the follies that are bread and wine
To Art's old foe, the wall-eyed Philistine,
That fatten those brute monsters dull and dense,
The Calibans of purblind Common-Sense,
And help my harpies, hovering under heaven,
To foul the fairest gifts that God has given. . . .

Enough, enough ! I 'm tired of all this musing ;
My thoughts are growing more and more confusing ;

Yes, the old torture of the mind is coming,

The old puzzles in mine ears again are drumming.

I, who have lived so many million ages,

Have found not out the riddles that these sages

Think they may solve in half-a-score of years,

In passing from their cradles to their biers;

And still they come like fever-dreams and madness

To crush me down in endless, hopeless sadness.

Some little satisfaction here I find ·

In gazing at these blind that lead the blind,

Some triumph—it is little, it is brief—

In poring o'er this Chaos of Belief. . .

I thank thee, Darwin! . . Those observant eyes

Saw men in monkeys, elephants in flies,

A crocodile in every cricket curled,

In every grain of dust a dædal world.

He saw, or thought he might with reason see;

Too strong that mind for swift credulity.

What with suspended judgment he had hinted

His weak disciples clutched with faith unstinted.

So Spencer philosophic fabrics based

On faint foundations trembling hands had traced ;

So Huxley to the rough mechanic tells

The hopeless creed wherewith his bosom swells ;

So Alpine Tyndall, icier than the Alps,

His scalpel lays upon the Bishops' scalps,

Excites the public rage in furious blast

By preaching down the preachers at Belfast,

Till, having ended his atomic mission,

He is evolved into a Politician ;

So every whipster now his morals shapes

By the high cult of atoms and of apes ;

Sweet vicars-choral of the Godless Church

Atomic anthems pipe at every porch,

Aggressive spinsters ape the Ape opinion,

And beardless freshmen boast themselves Darwinian.

God, Herbert Spencer, immortality,

All in one clearance overboard must fly. . .

O soothing creed ! . . But why does Spencer doubt ?

What ! after all the riddle's *not* found out ? . .

Whence came the atom whence all atoms come ?

What force set force in motion ? Nature's thumb !

By rule of thumb mechanic man was moulded,

By rule of thumb the worlds on worlds unfolded ! . .

It is an age that suits my humour well—

Jumble and tumble, everything pell-mell ;

An age *agnostic*, which with eager throat

Swallows new lies as old ones' antidote ;

Believes in palmistry and table-rappings

And demoniac wings of mystic flappings ;

Accepts the solar theory which unlocks

History's whole secret, with the help of Cox,

Who deems a revelation every yawn

Of mythic Müller blinking at the Dawn ;

Gulps esoteric Buddhism, and the Light

Of Asia in a European Night ;

Believes in that abstraction called "The People ;"

In Gladstone sheltering 'neath the Church's steeple;

In sonnets, roundels, and æstheticism;

In Drummond's scientific symbolism;

In Randolph Churchill; and in charlatanism;

In anarchy, and George, and nihilism;

In all the little lights and poetasters

A fleeting Fashion with its praises plasters;

In Whistler; and in Ruskin gone to seed;

In voters who have never learnt to read;

In women's right to look and live like men;

In the inspiration of Walt Whitman's pen;

In ruling rebel mobs without a rod;

In anything in Earth and Heaven but God.

An age of shams and mean mendacities

Through which the very fool they wheedle sees;

Of scandal-mongers prompting vice to scourge it,

To fleece the wicked world, but never purge it;

Of lies, invented just to float a journal,

Adopted as a regimen diurnal;

Of purity societies that hatch

The impurities they lie in wait to catch;

Of clubs established "for the People's good,"

That just supply their Secretaries' food;

Of philanthropic movements with an art in them

Of screening sins of ladies that take part in them;

Of social vice that only shocks Society

When brought to light and damned with notoriety;

Of Belgian and Parisian bestialities,

And viler sins of viler nationalities,

And every kind of deed that should be un-done,

Acclimatized in England's centre, London;

Of endless cheating and adulteration;

Of scoundrels drunk with public adulation;

Of guileless critics, and unbiassed Press;

Of honest merit crowned with sure success;

Of genius banned that never droops or dwindles;

Of gold-mines and innumerable swindles;

Of legislators glorying in the breaking

Of laws their very lives are spent in making;

Of babes their mothers are too fine to nurse,

And wives that deem their marriage-vows a curse.

An age when little boys of six are *blasé*

From hearing things the maids of their mammas
    say ;

When parents put to grass each "little treasure "

In order to be free to sin at leisure ;

When Youth believes it 's sharper than a knife

Because it knows the seamy side of life ;

When acts that merit our rebuking cloak we

From dread of getting tript by a *tu quoque ;*

When Parliament tears contracts up like paper,

And Justice flickers like a rushlight taper ;

When all who own must loss by Law endure,

And all securities are insecure ;

When servants itch to seize their master's places,

And all things governed kick against the traces. . .

Where are the heirs of that immortal band

Who strove to purer heights to lead their land,

Who dedicated art and skill and life

To Virtue's service in one ceaseless strife
With Evil, men who held a God of Light
Reigns o'er the vague and awful Infinite?
Who wears the armour now of Wilberforce?
Or who with Howard purges Misery's source?
Who now would rather die than prove a liar?
What martyr for his Christ would brave the fire?
What mummer mumbling "Stories of the Cross"
Would suffer for His sake a living's loss,
What ranter of Christ's pangs on Sabbath-morns
Bear one light skin-prick of His crown of thorns? . .

Ye sneer at honour, praise the schemer's sleekness,
And hold straightforwardness a childish weakness;
Contemn the hero though for you he dies,
And laud a crafty rascal to the skies;
Ay, kneel to every savage ye have warred on,
And to save Gladstone sacrifice a Gordon.
Void of belief in either God or Devil,
Each life 's a sordid strife or filthy revel;

No hope of Heaven and no fear of Hell

To prompt to good, from Evil's paths repel;

No vision of Eternity to fire

The spirit of man and lift him from the mire;

No hope of vaster life in boundless spheres

To consecrate the loves of mortal years.

Let each man live his little life of sin

Just far enough from Crime to save his skin,

Gain place or power or gold or gluttonous ease,

Crawl up to fame by any base degrees,

Eat, drink, and sleep, till, choked with London's
       fogs,

He dies unwept, to rot with apes and dogs! . .

Yet, were I dwelling in this world of mist,

I scarce could be an ultra-pessimist.

Hell's pessimism 's mortals' optimism;

If man, I'd lean to Sully's "meliorism."

For, ever through the weary circling years

I, struggling with the Power that sways the spheres,

I, the old Anarch, I that Chaos am,

I, the grim Wolf in clothing of the lamb,

I, subtil Serpent that through Eden crept,

Man's Enemy, whose hate hath never slept,

I, keen of eyes and base of heart, whose lot

Is to know Good and yet to choose it not,

I, Supreme Evil, who have warred on Good

Through age on age of horror and of blood,

I, who would mar the peace of Earth and Heaven,

Loose through the worlds Hell's thunders and its
      levin,

All order, beauty, joy in ruin lay,

Roll darkness upon light and night on day—

Ay me ! I feel my weakness in His grasp,

The knees that press my limbs, the palms that clasp,

A moment risen, am backward flung as dead,

And still the Victor's heel is on my head. . .

I know not for what end the Universe

Sustains me thus, who am its scourge and curse,

Why the Almighty with one final blow
Hath struck not and for ever laid me low.
Methinks it would be sweet to sleep.   Ah me,
Far sweeter than to strive perpetually
In failure, on through centuries of woe,
Foreknowing nothing save mine overthrow,
No higher joy than what a sneer may yield
At human foibles every hour revealed,
No hope of vaster triumph, richer gain,
Than just some increment of mortals' pain ! . .

So bestial Man appeareth from his birth,
So base in grain, so cumbered with his earth,
I marvel not that he so low can fall,
But that he soars so high, or soars at all.
But upward, onward still, in Hell's despite,
He struggles, yearning toward his gleam of light ;
The Good prevails, the surging floods of Sin,
Still threatening, still are held their bounds
        within ;

Earth's charioteer still curbs Earth's wanton steeds,

And guides them where the angel Virtue leads.

Ay, though I die not, Victor never yet

Have I my throne on Earth unshaken set,

Nor shall I while this orb about the sun

By the Invisible Hand in light is spun. . .

Eh, my good fellow? Once again the chair?

Have I not paid my penny? Pray, be fair ! . .

Well, I have lingered here perhaps too long.

Methinks I 've not escaped the prying throng.

That shrewd observer, yonder, turns again ;

He is a poet yet unknown to men.

The ladies, too, are gazing all together—

They smell a little sulphur in the breeze ;

They seem to search about for foot and feather,

And test me as they would a Stilton cheese.

Were they but certain of the thing I am,

I should not know on Earth one moment's calm.

Good Lord ! I should be plagued with invitations

To breakfasts, dances, cold and hot collations,

To *tête-à-têtes* and private conversations,

And amateur confessions, and ovations,

Afternoon-teas, and plays, and recitations,

And East End concerts, ritualist oblations,

Salvation armies, temperance orations,

Clerical meetings, ministerial dinners,

And mild retreats of melancholy sinners,

And crowded parties where you make your way

Half up the staircase ere the dawn of day;

And, by my faith, I'd rather lose my reason

Than be the Lion of a London Season. . .

But hark ! . . Time's up ! . . Farewell, my

children ! . . Pah ! . .

Ha ! ha ! ha ! ha ! ha ! ha ! ha ! ha ! ha ! ha !

THE END.

CHISWICK PRESS :--C. WHITTINGHAM AND CO., TOOKS COURT, CHANCERY LANE.

WORKS OF
GEORGE FRANCIS ARMSTRONG.

Opinions of the Press.

STORIES OF WICKLOW.

Fcap. 8vo. cloth, price 9s.

" His book is very welcome."—*Saturday Review.*

" These ' Stories of Wicklow' are all conceived and written in the true spirit of poetry. They abound in descriptions of natural scenery in which the eye and heart of the poet seem to be accompanied by the hand of the painter ; and they give forcible expression to some of the deepest and most complex feelings of the human breast. The passion of remorse, in conflict with other and more terrible passions, has seldom been more vividly depicted than in the grim story, ' The Wraith of De Riddles-ford's Castle.' ' The Fisherman,' which is stated to be a true narrative taken from the lips of a Wicklow seafarer, enshrines, with an altogether natural pathos, the loving sorrows of one of a class of men whose natures are often as tender as their lot is hard. Nearly all the poems in the volume are narratives, containing incidents which connect them with Wicklow; but the reader will find interest less in the events of the stories than in the descriptive and thoughtful passages which exalt the stories into poems. . . . The following is unexceptionable for its inspiration and its finished beauty of form."—*Academy.*

" Mr. Armstrong is a skilful and conscientious literary craftsman, and his hand has lost none of its cunning. Every poem in this volume is well wrought out, and is good in its degree. The author's blank verse is at once strong and supple. In lyrical measures his touch is firm and strong. . . . There is plenty of warmth, plenty of colour, much thought, and some humour. . . . He communicates to us a pervading sense of hill and lake, and brown, tumbling tarn,—he makes us breathe Wicklow air. . . . In our judgment, however, the special value of this book resides in those poems or passages which deal with the great scientific and theological problems of the day. ' Lugnaquillia ' is a delightful colloquial poem in blank verse, in which deep feeling and charming humour play into one another like light and shade. Many a man will start to find his unconscious ' religious convictions ' laid bare in the following lines. . . . Mr. Armstrong feels with great intensity those scientific and moral difficulties which are the special burden of this transitional age or stage. But he does not lose heart or hope. His hope, indeed, is not always sure and certain, but it is always deep-rooted and clinging. The opening section of 'De Verdun of Darragh,' though in it the author does not speak in his own person, may with safety be set down as the utterance of his personal thoughts. It is a lofty and impassioned defence of the reasonableness of those eternal hopes which the soul needs and will not let go. . . . Hardly any one who is weighed down by the burden of the age's problems could read this section, practically an independent whole, and other similar poems and passages in Mr. Armstrong's book, without feeling braced and cheered."—*Spectator.*

"From long excursions into the domains of Hebrew and classic poetry, Mr. George Francis Armstrong returns to the steep hills and green woodlands of Wicklow. Like Antæus, he seems to gain fresh vigour from contact with his native soil. . . . The 'sounds of tree and stream,' 'the clearness of the mountain air,' and 'the fragrance of the sea,' all mingle with the legends of the Wicklow glens and lakes. They make the book a delightful and inspiring companion for any one who loves to ramble, in the flesh or in the spirit, on dewy heights above the smoke and bustle of the work-a-day world. Another element is present, a pathetic undertone that is seldom absent from Irish poetry. In the blithest mood of the poet and his muse, there steal in, amid the sighing of the leaves and the noise of wind and waters, the 'voices of the Lost Ones,' and most of all the voice of his highly gifted brother, Edmund J. Armstrong, so often his companion in earlier climbs to the summit of Lugnaquillia, or in loiterings in Luggala, the 'Hollow of Sweet Sounds.' Of these metrical stories 'De Verdun of Darragh' is the longest; but there are others in the collection that may be preferred to it. 'The Fisherman,' 'The Wreck off Mizen-Head,' 'The Bursting of Lough Nahanagan,' and 'The Glen of the Horse,' are founded on local incidents or legends of comparatively recent date; in the latter three great skill is shown in adapting the rhythm to the stirring theme. In 'The Wraith of De Riddlesford's Castle,' a command of the gruesome is shown which Hoffman, or Bürger, or any other of the German masters of the horrible need not have disdained to own."—*Scotsman.*

"Mr. George Francis Armstrong's 'Stories of Wicklow' are most pleasant reading. Mr. Armstrong is already well known as the author of 'Ugone,' 'King Saul,' and other dramas, and his latest volume shows that the power and passion of his early work have not deserted him. Most modern Irish poetry is purely political, and deals with the wickedness of the landlords and the Tories, but Mr. Armstrong sings of the picturesqueness of Erin, not of its politics. He tells us very charmingly of the magic of its mists and the melody of its colour, and draws a most captivating picture of the peasants of county Wicklow. . . . The most ambitious poem in the volume is 'De Verdun of Darragh.' It is at once lyrical and dramatic. . . . All through it there is a personal and individual note."—*Pall Mall Gazette.*

"Let haste be made at once to express the most cordial agreement with the opinions enunciated melodiously in 'An Invocation,' and to assure the writer that the mountain-muse, with her waving hair and venturous mien, and tameless woodland ways, with her wild-wood flowers and garlands green, with sounds of stream and tree, with clearness of the mountain air and fragrance of the sea, is certainly far more likely to 'assuage the deeper want than seas of sensual art.' . . . In the mountain it is you must seek her, and to the mountain, after she has descended and exchanged sweet whispers with you, and breathed her inspiration into you, depend upon it she will ascend again. So at least, any muse that respects herself will be sure to do ; and so she will preserve her freshness, her vigour, her buoyancy. To this fact the author's own productions bear ample witness, whether he be telling a long romantic eventful tale, in four parts and in many varieties of lyric verse, or exhibiting his dashing powers of description, as in the piece entitled ' The Glen of the Horse,' or in the spirited lay of the flood and of the maiden rescued from death, or in the two parts of ' Luggalà,' or in other poems long or short."—*Illustrated London News.*

" By far the best poem is ' Luggalà,' a version of the world-old swan-legend, most picturesquely and sympathetically given in such Spenserian metre as it is seldom our good fortune to meet with ; the descriptions of natural scenery in this are really beautiful. . . . We have been charmed by ' Autumn Memories,' ' An Invitation,' and above all by ' Song-Time to Come.' In these Mr. Armstrong is seen at his best, as a tuneful and thoughtful lover of Nature."—*Graphic.*

" Mr. Armstrong's straightforward and vigorous writing is a refresh-ment after the sickly and introspective dreamings that most minor poets think fit to indulge in. The volume before us does not offer much that can well be quoted, as its strength lies in the narrative poems, which are full of rapidity and life, and extracts would give a very inadequate impression of them. But any one who wishes for exciting incidents well told, should read ' The Glen of the Horse,' or ' The Bursting of Lough Nahanagan.' Mr. Armstrong has the most genuine and irrepressible love of the scenes of his native district, and none can read his descrip-tions without catching some of his enthusiasm. He has the unfailing charm of reality. He writes of what he knows and loves, and does not pretend to any emotions that he has not really felt."—*Guardian.*

" Mr. Armstrong is undoubtedly one of our most versatile and finished poets. Themes classical and homely, elevated and commonplace, he has alike treated with felicity and finish. He has succeeded, too, in tragedy. His trilogy of Israelite dramas—' King Saul,' ' King David' and ' King Solomon '—is marked by rare force and variety. In the present case he has found subjects nearer home, amid localities endeared to him by residence and made familiar by many journeyings and rambles. No one could deny his vigour in narration. He touches the core of human nature here and there, . . . and relieves the narrative by reflection couched in glowing language. . . . This volume will undoubtedly add to Mr. Armstrong's reputation as a poet."—*Nonconformist.*

" Mr. Armstrong is a genuine poet. His sympathies with nature are strong, and his love for his Wicklow home intense. His opening invo-cation breathes all the freshness and loveliness of Wicklow scenery. The stories are always interesting, and for the most part of a very healthy tone."—*Tablet.*

" Mr. Armstrong is without doubt a poet ; and these ' Stories of Wicklow ' are both impressive and exhilarating productions. He belongs to a family in which poetry forms an essential element of existence. When he thinks he thinks in poetry. It is not possible for him that it should be otherwise. . . . Poems all more or less indicative of Mr. Arm-strong's fine poetic faculty and genius."—*Literary World.*

" Mr. Armstrong is better known to the poetry-reading public than is the author of either of the two works we have just reviewed, and these ' Stories of Wicklow ' will certainly maintain the reputation he has won among discriminating critics. Mr. Armstrong may ' claim applause of none ;' but whether he claims it or not, he will assuredly win it from those whose applause is best worth having. These romantic legends of Wicklow County are conceived so imaginatively, and told with such

passionate vividness and with such expressive music, that they take us
captive at once, hold us in their spell, and will not let us go until the
conclusion has been reached. Mr. Armstrong is a master of varied
versification. . . . He is always strong, sinewy and virile. His handling
of character and incident is admirable, and the book has therefore not
only an artistic but a strong human interest, the very thing which is so
markedly missing in so much of the poetry of the period."—*Manchester
Examiner.*

"This is a volume of stories told in verse, and the reader will find in
them a charm that irresistibly allures him on from stanza to stanza.
Mr. Armstrong ranks among the first of our living poets, and the reputation he has achieved is well sustained in these poems, which are rich in
mellow harmonies, graceful rhymes, graphically drawn scenes full of
swift and varied action, marked by the gloom of tragedy, the sunny rays
of light-hearted joyousness, and the tenderest and sweetest pathos. He
is a master of musical verse and something more. He possesses that
sympathy with man and nature without which no poet can move his
reader to a common confession of joy and sorrow. . . . In the other
'Stories' there are passages of equal beauty with those we have selected,
and altogether the volume is full of delightful reading."—*Liverpool
Courier.*

"'Stories of Wicklow'. . are told in flowing verse. . . 'The Wraith
of De Riddlesford's Castle'. . tells of the fearful remorse and the dis-
ordered imagination which peoples the air with accusing shapes when
unlawful love has culminated in murder. It is hardly possible to read
the story without a creeping of the flesh. . . Although all the selections
breathe deep sentiment, the one to which special reference has been
made is solitary in its superlative gruesomeness."—*Liverpool Daily Post.*

"'The Glen of the Horse' is a spirited ballad of the terrible death of
a mounted rebel chased over a precipice in the Wicklow mountains by
his pursuer, who found too late that the enemy he had ridden to death
was a friend of former years, and his kinswoman's betrothed. This poem,
and 'The Bursting of Lough Nahanagan,' are founded on fact, as also is
'The Fisherman' a simple but pathetic tale of the sea. . . . The finest
poems in the volume are 'The Wraith of De Riddlesford's Castle'—a
romantic ghost-story of the good old-fashioned style, containing some
really thrilling incidents and scenes of spectral horror—and 'Luggalà,' an
Irish-Keltic fairy story of an Argonaut-like voyage in search of a land of
rest beyond the sunset, one of those charming Swan-legends that delight
old and young alike. The poem is filled with rich and beautiful passages.
. . . These poems glow with a patriotic love for his Wicklow mountains and
glens, the scenery of which he here depicts. . . . His language throughout is graceful, his verse always unexceptionable in rhyme and rhythm,
no mean achievement in these days, when there is so much bad 'prose
and worse.'"—*Birmingham Gazette.*

"Mr. George Francis Armstrong's 'Stories of Wicklow' will maintain
the reputation which former poetical works have gained him, and which
was shared by his brother Edmund, whose biographer and literary
executor he has been. These new Stories are mostly narratives in
varied metre, and are marked by a strong love of Nature, a lively fancy,
and an elevation of thought and tone."—*Leeds Mercury.*

"This is a volume of genuine poetry, full of stately music, noble
thoughts, and genuine passion. It would be a mercy to admirers of
Walt Whitman to submit them to the influence of a poet like this by
reading one of these volumes to them aloud. Here is no hurry, no
coarseness of epithet or vulgarity of idea, no straining after effect or

singularity, but genius under the perfect control of sanity, and polish without weakness. We recommend all lovers of poetry of the first class to this glorious book."—*Sheffield Independent.*

" In 'The Glen of the Horse' we have a vigorous rendering of the legend that haunts the valley of Glenmalure—a legend in itself terrible in pathos—and although it would be unjust even to seem to disparage the poet's deeper, subtler verse, we commend it to the general reader as stirring the blood and moving the sympathies. To avoid comparison we refrain from selecting other individual contributions for particular mention, and will content ourselves with the general observation that the poems are of exceptional excellence, and that while some more than others impress us with their superlative merit, there is no instance in which good qualities can fail to be discerned. The collection will be widely read . . . hereafter perhaps the book may be presented at a cheaper cost. One hopes as much, because a good book cannot be too extensively distributed."—*Western Daily Mercury.*

" In a volume of over 400 pages, G. F. Armstrong gives us some delightful verses in which the brilliant and thoughtful writer, who a few years ago gave us an unfading 'Garland from Greece,' surpasses even that most finished collection of Lyrics. The title of the new volume is ' Stories of Wicklow.' The leading poem is a descriptive piece, ' De Verdun of Darragh,' which is as full of rich harmonies as it is varied in metre and cadence. 'The Glen of the Horse' is graphically and powerfully written. One of the gems of the collection, ' The Living and the Dead,' we have already printed in *The Courant.* In poetic narration, in vivid description of scenery, and in the art and mastery of language some of the pieces are exquisitely beautiful, and cannot fail to add to the solid reputation of the writer."—*Newcastle Courant.*

" Mr. George Francis Armstrong is one of the most pleasing, musical and graceful of our modern poets, and admirers of his verse will welcome these 'Stories of Wicklow,' poems which, though not, like the ' Garland from Greece,' speaking with the warmth and richness and colour of a southern clime, are yet marked by the same love of Nature, and by the same power of sympathizing with and portraying her many-changing moods. There is a breezy freshness about Mr. Armstrong's verse which, in these days of second-hand and pumped-up enthusiasm, is very grateful to one's susceptibilities. He sings of the rivers and lakes, the woods and the heaths, the valleys and the mountain-peaks, the jutting headlands, and the storm-beaten coasts of his native Wicklow. He sings as one who knows them well, and by the sympathetic spell of his genius he brings his readers to love them also."—*Nottingham Daily Guardian.*

" The product of a poetically constituted mind of the first order. The author . . . belongs to a literary family who have splendidly contributed to the great Republic of Letters. . . . Mr. George Francis Armstrong is a sincere lover of his country, as his 'Stories of Wicklow' abundantly prove. . . . He is a student of human nature, but of external nature as well, and the latter he loves very truly, and his study is profound and appeals directly to the heart. These 'Stories of Wicklow' are the product of a wayfarer, wandering amidst the loveliest hills and dales of Ireland, filled with the rarest fancies that their exquisite scenic grandeur could beget. . . . He is a painter from nature, and owes to nature the best part of his inspiration. He had rather sing *her* music. His poetry is spontaneous. . . . These 'Stories of Wicklow' are enchanting to every reader. They are inspired by the rarest spirit of poetry, and appeal in particular to the native sentiment."—*Irish Times.*

"His work proves him no minor poet, but abounding in the perpetual beauty, the unfailing metrical charm, the enduring enthusiasm, the temperance, wisdom, and moral goodness that only the great poets possess. .... This volume should be treasured while there is anyone to be proud of the true glories of Ireland, while there are lovers of true poetry and of what is best in Man and Nature."—*Dublin University Review.*

"He has given us a Garland from Ireland worthy and more than worthy to match with his 'Garland from Greece.' In the volume before us there is at least one tragedy—'Altadore'—more affecting than the author's Hebrew Trilogy. That he should have gathered such a harvest from Irish soil to-day is a wonder to be ranked with Horrocks's Observation of the Transit of Venus amid the commotions of Charles I.'s time. ... We think the present volume places Mr. Armstrong very high indeed among the poets of the Victorian age."—*Dublin Evening Mail.*

"Here we have traditions old and new, tales of modern life, descriptions of scenery, and the bracing and joyous rambles of loving friends; some of the poems long and elaborate, others consisting of a stanza or two of simple spontaneous emotion, mere breaths of poetry, as brief as the windflaw that runs purpling over the level sea on a day of perfect calm, or that in 'trancèd summer nights,' passes through the woods in a single sigh. ... We hope our readers will regret that we are unable to give more varied examples of the lofty and passionate poetry of this noble volume. Not a phase of the loveliness of the Wicklow glens and seas but will be found portrayed there, and associated with thoughts and images that make it even dearer than before."—*Irish Fireside.*

"The author is one of the most prolific of later English poets. .... His previous books have been much praised by competent British critics. In this book he treats of a variety of themes, and in many metres. One is impressed by his facility, and a capacity for descriptive writing which is apparent throughout his work. ... They are all gracefully written."— *Boston (U.S.A.) Herald.*

"The political condition of Ireland makes it inevitable that the lyre attuned to national themes shall evoke the quickest response from the popular heart. But the true realm of the poet is larger than any country; his place is above the world, whence he may see all that is in it, not merely a part. It is well to make the songs of a people, but it is also well to give poetical voice to the emotions, passions and aspirations of mankind. Mr. Armstrong's poetry belongs in the main to what is generally acknowledged to be the higher order of verse. .... The 'Stories of Wicklow' are better calculated to make Mr. Armstrong known among his own countrymen than any of his previous productions. The stories are full of interest, and the descriptions of places and scenery are admirable. ... This book alone, if the others had never appeared, would be sufficient to stamp Mr. Armstrong as a true poet. ... What would be called in stage phrase the scenic effects of all these poems are rich, harmonious and vivid. There appears to be hardly a spot in Wicklow which the poet does not know, and he has the rare gift of being able to make others see with his own eyes. His descriptions of places are as remarkable for detail (always difficult in verse) as for their completeness as finished pictures. ... In one respect Mr. Armstrong's verse differs from that of nearly all other Irish poets. Nothing in its form or style indicates the nationality of the writer. In quality, however, it ranks among the best poetry of the present time, and it cannot fail to be enjoyed by all persons of good literary taste. It is fresh, vigorous, and varied, and it has the special merit of not possessing any of the characteristics of the hasty, exotic school, which has found too much success in England, and been imitated to some extent in America. It is all clean, and fit for the young as well as for the old to read."—*Boston (U.S.A.) Pilot.*

"M. Armstrong abonde en descriptions éclatante et finement nuancées, en effusions lyriques d'un magnifique essor. Et son vers ne le trahit pas ; se prétant aux rhythmes les plus variés, il reste toujours ample, élégante et cadencé. Fasciné par les merveilleux spectacles de cette terre et enflammé d'une foi ardente le poète a puisé aux sources les plus pures de l'inspiration : la Nature et Dieu. A chaque page, ses strophes ailées, qui viennent de nous peindre quelque ravissante vision et de prêter une voix à la création muette, s'en volent sans effort vers une région plus lumineuse encore et nous entretiennent du Créateur, de sa providence, de la vie future. M. Armstrong est un vrai poète : il joint à la délicatesse des sentiments et à l'élévation de la pensée, la richesse du coloris et la perfection de la forme."—*Polybiblion* (Paris).

VICTORIA REGINA ET IMPERATRIX.

A JUBILEE SONG FROM IRELAND, 1887.

"Mr. G. F. Armstrong's *Victoria*, a 'Jubilee Song from Ireland,' takes high rank among the many odes and hymns that celebrate what ought to be an inspiring event with our poets. It is finely modulated and distinguished by a sustained elevation of sentiment that befits the dignity of the theme."—*Saturday Review.*

"There seems something especially graceful in a Jubilee song of exultant loyalty which comes from County Wicklow. Such is Mr. George F. Armstrong's 'Victoria,' a poem vigorous and musical in expression, and breathing a lofty spirit of pride in faithful allegiance to Her Majesty. Mr. Armstrong's merits as a poet of strength and skill have been exhibited in a series of stirring works, but if evidence of them were wanting, it would be found in abundance in his fine Jubilee ode."—*Scotsman.*

"The 'Song' is, in fact, an ode, and full of elegant passages in measures appropriate to that form. This is indeed one of the most successful celebrations of the Jubilee in verse."—*Globe.*

"This Jubilee Ode, composed near Bray, on the mountain shore of Wicklow, whence he sees the mountains of North Wales, appeals to the heart of every true Briton with the expresed consciousness of a patriotism shared by loyal men on both sides of St. George's Channel. The 'Wild Harp of Erin' makes good music in this strain. It is fine in thought, in diction, and in versification."—*Illustrated London News.*

"A book, the author of which is already known as a poet of marked ability, and who now worthily represents the loyal spirit which recognizes with gratitude the obligations of Ireland, and breathes its aspirations for the welfare of that country under the rule of our Gracious Queen."—*Queen.*

"It differs from the poems on the same theme by some other distinguished writers of verse, inasmuch as it will not detract from the high reputation of its author."—*Christian Leader.*

"It is decidedly refreshing to find that even the 'Wild Harp of Erin' has strings, which can be touched in sympathy with that wave of loyalty which has just passed over our kingdom. . . . Versatile and finished, Mr. Armstrong never sinks to anything approaching the commonplace, and here, as in other works, he is at home in his beloved country which passionately inspires him.". . .—*Bristol Times.*

"George Francis Armstrong, whose poems, 'A Garland from Greece,' and 'Stories of Wicklow,' placed him in the front rank of living poets, has written a Jubilee Song from Ireland. . . . It is written in the form of an ode, and characterized by all the remarkable vigour and precision of expression of his best work. This Jubilee ode should more than maintain the high reputation Mr. Armstrong's preceding poems gained for him."—*Newcastle Courant.*

"Mr. George Francis Armstrong's Jubilee Ode is a work of a very different class from those we have noticed. They are necessarily of but ephemeral interest. It deserves to live, and we trust will live. . . . Mr. Armstrong has written much that is worth reading, but he has never written a piece of more eloquent declamation than this Jubilee Ode."—*Daily Express* (Dublin).

"There is much spirit and high sentiment in this poem, and it will compare favourably with the best that has appeared under the muse's inspiration."—*Manchester Courier.*

"It is earnestly to be desired that Mr. George Francis Armstrong's poem 'Victoria' may be read by every well-wisher to Ireland. . . . True poetry is lasting and will live when Jubilees are forgotten. This poem of Mr. Armstrong's deserves to live and be remembered. . . . Mr. Armstrong is that happy combination—a true poet and a true Irishman."—*Nottingham Guardian.*

"Mr. Armstrong's masterly ode, an opportune and welcome addition to the Jubilee literature of this Jubilee year of grace."—*Allen's Indian Mail.*

"The offering is certainly an attractive one, both as to its sentiments and its poetry. . . . He has exhibited true poetic genius and enthusiastic loyal feeling, and these two qualities are enough to give a high value to his Jubilee offering."—*Sydney Morning Herald* (Australia).

"An ode which breathes a very lofty and loyal spirit, and therefore is doubly welcome as coming from Ireland. . . . Of all the Jubilee odes it is by far the best tribute that has been paid to-day

'To her who through the fifty summers flown,
Has worn her lucid diadem unstained.'"
—*Melbourne Argus.*

"Of all native attempts to celebrate the event in verse, Mr. Armstrong's song from Ireland is decidedly the best, as it is undoubtedly the most ambitious."—*Dublin Evening Mail.*

"Among the many poems which have been inspired by Her Majesty's Jubilee, by no means the least honour must be paid to Mr. George Francis Armstrong's 'Jubilee Song from Ireland.' This song is an admirable composition, and will further increase Mr. Armstrong's reputation."—*Northern Whig* (Belfast).

WORKS OF
GEORGE FRANCIS ARMSTRONG.

A GARLAND FROM GREECE.

Fcap. 8vo , cloth, price 9s.

"Mr. Armstrong maintains, and even improves, his position among the English poets of the day . . . . No writer of the time, except Mr. Matthew Arnold—and, if we are to take his 'Transcripts' into account, of course, Mr. Browning—has so thoroughly imbibed the classical spirit."—*Spectator.*

"We may confidently recommend the volume to all readers who may wish to realize so much of physical Greece as a book may convey. The variety of subjects and treatment is remarkable. But nowhere does Mr. Armstrong appear otherwise than at his ease . . . . Mr. Armstrong is under the marked influence of no particular school. His writing possesses individuality both of thought and expression, and he has at his command an abundant flow of melodious verse . . . . A very charming volume."—*Pall Mall Gazette.*

"It consists of a medley of poems, all dealing with the subject of Greece from topographical, historical, legendary, political, and other points of view. As might be expected, the legendary and antique poems are the best, especially 'Selemnos,' a poem which would give more than one good subject to an artist, and the 'Closing of the Oracle.' All the book is scholarly and thoroughly readable."—*Academy.*

"Mr. Armstrong has drawn enthusiasm from several sources. The actual scenery of Greece does not seem to impress him with the sense of desolation which it produces on some spectators. He is enthusiastically Phil-Hellenic as to the present inhabitants of the country ; and he has the classical sympathies and associations which might be expected from a cultivated Englishman. These various motives find expression by turns in his verse."—*Athenæum.*

"A delightful book . . . . A large part of the merit of this work lies in the choice of subjects ; but the treatment is very vigorous, and the 'Brigand of Parnassus' and 'The Last Sortie from Mesolonghi' are especially fine . . . . There is one poem which is not of Greek origin, but has an extraordinary depth of analysis and emotion ; it is entitled 'Time the Healer.'"- *New York Evening Post.*

"Whatever may be the subject dealt with, it is always treated with delicacy and taste. The reader feels that not only is the local colouring true, that the places alluded to are accurately as well as picturesquely described, but that the characters introduced are real flesh and blood, and not merely lay-figures in a Greek dress . . . . A volume of poetry

which may not only be glanced at, but studied, with pleasure."—
Edinburgh Courant.

"Mr. George Francis Armstrong's name and works will be familiar to
all real students of the English poets of the day. He is the author of
several volumes of really noble lyric and dramatic poems, which in the
opinion of the judicious hold a far higher place than a great deal of verse
that happening to be in accord with the superficial moods of the time,
commands a greater temporary popularity . . . . Graceful word-pictures
of Greek scenery, echoes and versions of old myths, and stirring ballads
and tales in verse of the struggles of the modern Hellenes with their
Mussulman oppressors, make up its contents. Mr. Armstrong employs
many metres and shows himself a master of them all."—*Scotsman.*

"[He] has long been placed high amongst living poets by all who can
appreciate earnest thought and a worthy choice of subjects wedded to
thoroughly good technical treatment . . . . Contains some of the
Author's finest work . . . . Hardly any praise could be excessive for
such musical and stirring songs as the 'Agoyat' and the 'Klepht's
Flight' . . . . 'The Death of Epicurus' must be *read;* selections from
this noble poem could only do it injustice . . . . These lines have not
been surpassed by any living writer."—*Graphic.*

"A volume of poems from Mr. Armstrong is always sure of a welcome
in the literary world. [He] has so often and so successfully proved his
power of producing strong and musical verse appealing directly to the
highest poetic sentiment, that his claim to distinguished notice amongst
contemporary poets cannot be disregarded."—*Irish Times.*

"The present volume has merits quite distinctive and exceptional.
But for the occasional apostrophes to England, the love of English
ideals, and the purity of the English idiom we might take the book for
the work of a native Greek . . . . Old tales and legends are charmingly
revived in 'The Satyr,' 'Orithyia' and 'Selemnos;' Marathon and
Chæronea receive their meed of loyal remembrance; and the modern
struggles of the Greeks for liberty are fitly pictured and sung in the
'Brigand of Parnassus,' 'The Last Sortie from Mesolonghi,' and 'The
Chiote.' With nature as with man the poet feels a full and friendly
sympathy, and the humblest phases of the world's life are reflected in his
song."—*Boston (N.S) Literary World.*

POEMS: Lyrical and Dramatic.

A New Edition. Fcap. 8vo., cloth, price 6s.

"Mr. G. F. Armstrong, whose genuine poetical abilities have still, we
hope, to bear good and lasting fruit, has re-issued his 'Poems Lyrical and
Dramatic,' for the most part early works, full of the exuberant promise
and vitality of youth."—*Guardian.*

"Son livre le fait connaître pour un esprit sincère, profondément reli-
gieux, mais n'accordant sa confiance à aucune des églises ou des sectes de
son pays, pour un cœur aimant qui s'épanchait dans des vers plutôt ten-
dres que passionnés."—*Revue des Deux Mondes.*

UGONE : A TRAGEDY.

A New Edition.   Fcap. 8vo., cloth, price 6s.

" We notice with pleasure a new edition of this tragedy, which has been vigorously conceived, and written with sustained spirit and elegance . . . The explanations in the closing scene are spontaneous and thoroughly animated, the circumstances have been judiciously prepared, and the spectacle becomes absorbing and magnificent."—*Pall Mall Gazette.*

" A composition of really remarkable performance and of genuine promise."—*Saturday Review.*

KING SAUL.

(THE TRAGEDY OF ISRAEL, PART I.)

Fcap. 8vo., cloth, price 5s.

" The violent, but always unsuccessful, efforts of remorse to find oblivion in a deliberate attitude of defiance, the sense of the hollowness of kingship when severed from the reality of influence, and the king's still eager love of his people, though blurred always by despair, and sometimes by the brute impulse of impotent jealousy against the foredestined successor, have been taken up one after another in Mr. Armstrong's drama in a really masterly manner . . . . We can scarcely find a higher commendation for the tragedy of ' King Saul' than to say that in choosing his subject its author did not overtax his legitimate strength."—*Saturday Review.*

KING DAVID.

(THE TRAGEDY OF ISRAEL, PART II.)

Fcap. 8vo., cloth, price 6s.

" There can be no doubt as to the imaginative vigour, and persistent intellectual power with which Mr. Armstrong pursues his task . . . . The sequence of events sweep along in his pages with a grand impressive roll, having the deep music of passion and imagination for an appropriate accompaniment."—*Guardian.*

" Mr. Armstrong's right to be numbered among our poets is conceded." -*Sunday Times.*

KING SOLOMON.

(THE TRAGEDY OF ISRAEL, PART III.)

Fcap. 8vo., cloth, price 6s.

" Dramatic poems which can claim to have captivated the critics, not of this country only, but of France, Germany, and America."—*Edinburgh Review.*

" There can be no doubt that this is in various ways a production displaying genuine power and original thought . . . . A vivid dramatic poem, dealing with various problems of human passion, suffering, and trial. The language and often the ideas, are entirely modern, but this only helps to bring out the essential humanity of the men before us, and the reality of their flesh and blood."—*Saturday Review.*

" To the energy of purpose necessary to approach and grapple with a theme so gigantic, there has been joined a patience in execution which has allowed of no slovenly work to the best of its judgment ; no mean skill in the mechanism of verse ; a fancy fertile in conceptions which not seldom reach grandeur ; and a remarkable descriptive faculty . . . . ' King Solomon ' is in the portraiture of the hero the best of the three plays."— *Academy.*

" Quite uncommon mastery of language and much melody of versification distinguish it [' The Tragedy of Israel ']. For energy of rhetoric, for the really poetical beauty of the lyrical portions of it, for the richness of imagery which adorns, even over-adorns it throughout, it takes high rank among the poems of the present day."—*Spectator.*

" We must designate the attested powers of the poet as extraordinarily great—so elevated is his imagination ; so full of idealism his representation of powerful emotions ; and, finally, so perfectly beautiful his language."—*Magazin für die Literatur des Auslandes* (Berlin).

" Poëte comme son frère Edmund, mort il y a quelques années, M. G. F. Armstrong s'était fait connaitre par un recueil de *Poëmes lyriques et dramatiques* et par une tragédie d'*Ugone*, quand il donna *le Roi Saul*, qui a justement augmenté sa réputation, accrue encore par *le Roi David* et *le Roi Salomon.*"—*Polybiblion* (Paris).

" As contributions to modern classics these work are destined to hold high rank and be universally admired."—*Boston (U. S.) Commonwealth.*

THE LIFE AND LETTERS OF EDMUND

J. ARMSTRONG.

Fcap. 8vo., with Portrait and Vignette.   Price 7s. 6d.

" There was a fulness of life, and of Irish life, in Edmund Armstrong, of which the years he lived afford no measure. . . . . The faculties, elements, and activities which went with it were very various ; it was a life abounding in happiness and hope, with seasons of gloom and sore disturbance ; abounding in loves and admirations—love and admiration of nature, love and admiration of books, and other and still more passionate loves and admirations ; full of reflection and emotion, giving out at one time

> ' Hyblæan murmurs of poetic thought,
> Industrious in its joy ; '

Giving birth at another to battles of the spiritual instincts with their intellectual persecutors and destroyers ; and passing through all forms and phases of belief, unbelief, disbelief, and misbelief, though happily finding its way at last to faith and peace. . . . . In the biographies of these times the merit of all merits which is rarest is ' the tender grace of not too much.' To this merit, as well as many others, the biography of Edmund Armstrong may fairly lay claim. . . . . His life was a poem."—*Edinburgh Review.*

" His life had in it material enough for two lives of the same length—frolics of boyhood, the growth of a passion for external nature, ardent friendship, an unsatisfied love, the loss and restoration of a faith, authorship in prose and verse, all these filled to the full the narrow count of his years. . . . . The editor has done his work well, with all reverence and love for his dead brother, and with many lively and tender touches of his own."—*Academy.*

" Mr. George Francis Armstrong's memoir of this remarkable youth is full of deep interest for all who care to follow the mental throes and experience of a nature at once highly intellectual and exceedingly emotional —its struggles towards development, its yearnings and efforts in search of truth. . . . . It is the growth of his mind, the influences under which it was shaped, and the processes through which it passed which his brother depicts with a literary grace all the more enjoyable because of its entire freedom from artificiality, and with a sympathy and insight inspired by his deep affection for his subject."—*Scotsman.*

" Armstrong had a varied, turbulent soul-life within himself, and he could truly be ranked with those among whom Georges Sand's happy remark finds application, ' Il y a des gens qui vivent beaucoup à la fois et dont les ans comptent double ' . . . . By the adoption of many of the charming original letters of the deceased, George Armstrong has, as far as the construction was possible, fashioned an autobiography out of a biography ; and by this means he has attained his object, to give the reader a vital picture of the poet. We fancy that we see before us the highly-gifted youth, to whom in an unusual measure it was given to awaken interest and sympathy, and make himself the centre of a circle of loving friends. His joyous inspiration works contagiously through his vivacity, and his nimble, merry fancy brings us in a moment from tears to laughter ; while on the other hand the daring with which his youthful spirit plunged into the darkest depths of the human soul, and the fortitude with which he bore severe bodily suffering, fill us with true reverence."— *Magazin für die Literatur des Auslandes* (Berlin).

EDITED BY THE SAME AUTHOR.

THE POETICAL WORKS OF EDMUND J. ARMSTRONG.

A New Edition, containing many Poems not before published. Fcap. 8vo., with Portrait on Steel by C. H. Jeens, and Vignette.   Price 5s.

"Of course his powers in descriptive as well as in other poetry are seen to more advantage in his twenty-first than in his eighteenth year ; and a few lines from ' The Prisoner of Mount Saint Michael,' written in 1863, will show not only his gifts in that kind, but something more. . . . The impressions from nature in such passages as these are skilfully interposed to afford the reader a short and very needful rest in the somewhat headlong course of a tumultuously tragic story ; and in this the skill is seen in the rhythm as well as in the change of scene.   There could hardly be found elsewhere an example of blank verse written at so early an age with such happy measurements in its structure, and with movements so easy and so graceful. . . . . The story is wildly frightful, but not at all beyond the bounds of what human nature can find room for in the way of possible guilt and crime on the part of the heroine, and possible weakness and bewilderment on the part of her lover. . . . . As a plot for a melodrama no story could be better. . . . The power evinced [in its treatment] is very rare ; and it may be observed with equal truth that in these days the skill by which a good story is constructed is also rare. . . . . Into the extant lyrical poems of Edmund Armstrong—the extant *miscellaneous* lyrical, that is—as well as into the non-extant dramatic, the element of humour found its way ; not, however, into those which are lyrical in the stricter sense, not into the songs.   These spring from an unmixed emotion, simple and sad ; and as in the case of Kingsley (to whose noble nature and wide range of faculties and feelings those of Armstrong have rather a singular resemblance), his saddest songs may be said to be born of the sea ; and his saddest are, of course, his sweetest." *Edinburgh Review.*

" Lyrical, dramatic, and narrative, they exhibit considerable mastery of verse ; they betray a passionate temperament (often craving repose) and a vigorous, if sometimes unchastened, imagination."—*Academy.*

" Poems lit by the fire of genius, beautiful in form, deep and lofty in thought, and displaying especially that intense love of nature and enjoyment of her mysteries and charms, the possession of which in full measure is accorded only to very few. . . . . Of the poems the longest and most ambitious is the ' Prisoner of Mount Saint Michael,' a wild story of passion and crime, which is full of unmistakable power.   But it is in some of his shorter poems and lyrics that Armstrong's genius is most fully revealed."--*Scotsman.*

" Among these [poems] ' The Prisoner of Mount Saint Michael ' stands preëminent.   It is a narrative in blank verse. . . . . The conflicting passions are powerful and vivid, but also tender and rich in sensitiveness. Some descriptive passages, especially descriptions of landscape, are very delicate.   A melodious tone runs through the whole. . . . . Every verse of his breathes healthfulness, and has an effect as refreshing—a rarity in this age."--*Magazin für die Literatur des Auslandes* (Berlin).

ESSAYS AND SKETCHES OF EDMUND J. ARMSTRONG.

Fcap. 8vo., price 5*s*.

"The prose is the prose of a poetical mind. And it is the more and not the less poetical in being free from the incongruous embellishments which so often force their way into the prose of youthful poets. . . . . [In the essay on 'Essay-writing'] he exemplifies, whilst he teaches the principles by which an essayist should be guided. . . . . Young as the teacher was, his teachings are not juvenile. And in some of the essays which follow the disquisitions on essay-writing, though they are of earlier dates, the practice of the author does not stand far apart from the principles he inculcates. . . . . Those on the life and writings of Coleridge and the writings of Wordsworth may be conjectured to belong to the author's latter years ; and if the love and admiration of books is, as has been said, to be numbered amongst the abounding loves and admirations by which Armstrong's life was enriched and animated, assuredly his love and admiration for these two great men may be regarded as of all such sentiments the most fervently felt as well as the most deeply founded. But Shelley, Keats, Goethe, and Edgar Poe have each their ample share. And the life of each poet is considered in relation to his works, without bringing the mortal to bear too heavily upon the immortal part, or mixing too much the flowers and the fruits with the earth from which they spring."—*Edinburgh Review.*

" His prose-writings are very interesting. Most of them are critical essays. . . . . There is abundant evidence of the extent of his culture, his candour, his subtlety of thought, and his faculty of critical insight. The essays on Coleridge, Shelley, and Wordsworth, for example, will well repay study, while their style is singularly vigorous and polished."
—*Scotsman.*

LONDON: LONGMANS AND CO.

www.ingramcontent.com/pod-product-compliance
Lightning Source LLC
Chambersburg PA
CBHW020800020726
47495CB00008B/2518